A Vineyard Vow

The Vineyard Sunset Series

Katie Winters

Chapter One

Amanda had a thing about lists. Like her mother before her, Amanda liked to see all her next steps in front of her: what to pick up at the grocery store, which law school assignments were due when, and who to send a birthday card to. To her, this meant she had control.

Now, seated on the carpet in front of the splendor of her Christmas tree, Amanda found herself composing a very different sort of list.

1. Rutgers University Law School - graduate in three and a half years

2. Marriage at age 22 (January)

3. Starter house, age 23 (at least three-bedroom)

4. First child, two years after law school ends (possible names: Clinton? Winnie?)

5. ?

Five. What could five be? Amanda furrowed her brow and stitched the back end of the pen into her chin. Admittedly, this early evening, she had already drunk a glass of merlot, and her mind was fuzzy with a mix of apprehension and excitement.

This list had nothing to do with the fact that she and her fiancé, Chris, needed more pepper for the pepper shaker. It had nothing to do with stopping at the gas station across town because it was five cents cheaper per gallon. Nope. It had everything to do with life— and Amanda's plan to do everything by the book.

She was ready. She'd taken charge of it years before. And here it was, stretched out before her— a list of days, months, and years of happiness and prosperity.

Her phone pinged. She stretched a long, slender arm out to grab it. She found an email reflected back when she lifted it— one with the subject line: RUTGERS LAW SCHOOL SEMESTER GRADES.

Her heart pounded. She hadn't anticipated receiving her semester GPA until some time after the first of the year. With her belly churning, she forced herself to open the message, head to the administrative website, and seek her grades.

As the website loaded, she considered the previous six months of her life, which had been spent between class halls at Rutgers Law School, her apartment, and Martha's Vineyard, where her mother had moved in the wake of her grandfather's dementia diagnosis and her divorce from Amanda's father. It had probably been the most chaotic year of Amanda's life— and she had struggled at times to funnel her focus into her schoolwork.

"You shouldn't spend so much time there," Chris had said a few times regarding the Vineyard. "Your life is here. Your job is school. You'd hate yourself if you messed it all up for a few extra nights with your mom."

The words had stung.

As a rule, of course, Amanda loved her fiancé, Chris, more than any other creature on the planet. But her mother? Her mother was part-guardian angel, part-superwoman. She'd only just beaten breast cancer; she had fallen in love all over again with her high school sweetheart; and she had the bravery to go out there and get what she needed in this life.

She seemed to grow stronger with every new day that passed.

Amanda sometimes wondered if she would have that kind of strength as a forty-four-year-old woman. She prayed she would.

In any case, when Chris had suggested that she spent too much time on the Vineyard, she had simply ignored him. It wasn't as though he'd wanted to wrong her. He had her and their relationship's best interests at heart.

Okay. Here it was: her semester grade. She typed her password into the system, waited with bated breath, and then shrieked to high heavens when she gazed at the screen.

A 3.78 GPA.

Not. Freaking. Bad.

She leaped to her feet and did a little dance near the Christmas tree. She felt electric, overcharged, and she sipped back the rest of her wine and poured herself another glass. All her life, she had longed to be a criminal lawyer like her mother and father. All her life, she'd wanted to succeed.

And one semester's high GPA was one step closer to that.

Amanda nibbled on a leftover Christmas cookie and hovered over the counter as she pressed her phone to her ear. Chris's phone blared six rings before it cut out. She pressed her lips together in a straight line, surprised and then tried again. It was just past six, which meant that Chris's job had probably already let him go for the night. That said, it wasn't so uncommon that they held him back— especially as they were short-staffed over the holidays.

Finally, Chris answered on the fourth ring. "What's up, babe?"

Amanda's heart flipped around. She had always loved Chris's voice. It was gritty and powerful and somehow a reminder of this strong, wonderful man she would soon marry and then have children with. She could hardly stand how much she loved him.

"Hey! Chris! Gosh, um. I have some news!"

There was silence on the other end of the line. After a moment, there was a muffled voice in the background, then another. Amanda's lips curved downward.

It wasn't his fault that she wanted his attention right then and he couldn't give it. It wasn't his fault at all.

"Hey, babe, sorry about that," Chris said. "It's a little chaotic here."

"I'm sorry to hear that," Amanda replied. If there was anything she was, it was understanding. It was sort of her thing.

"What did you say about news?"

"I have something I want to tell you! I was thinking I could make a nice dinner and um. Yeah."

Again, there was a muffled voice in the background. Amanda still couldn't make out what was said.

"Dinner? Sure. That sounds great."

"Any requests?"

"Hmm." He clucked his tongue for a second. "Eggplant parmesan."

Amanda laughed good-naturedly. "With garlic bread?"

"You know me too well."

"You're easy," Amanda said.

They chuckled together for a moment. Amanda breathed a soft sigh of relief. There they were: back to their old, easy ways. Amanda and Chris, Chris and Amanda. Together forever—everyone knew that.

"Okay, so you'll be back in about an hour or so, or?"

"Yeah. Around that, yeah," Chris affirmed. "Not too much later."

"Okay." Amanda walked toward the fridge to hunt for eggplants. "I love you, Chris."

"And I love you, Amanda Harris."

"Not Harris for long," Amanda stated. "You're taking my good name away from—"

But at that moment, silence rang through the speaker. She blinked down at the phone to find that Chris had hung up. She shook it off; after all, he was busy with something and needed time with his colleagues before he slid out for the day. He had been away for Christmas and had grown increasingly anxious about his time away. They'd even put off their honeymoon for summertime to ensure that they could get back from Martha's Vineyard and dive back into law school and Chris's work.

Whatever it was that Chris did, Amanda was never so clear on it. It had something to do with importing and exporting. He took many business clients out to eat and drink; he was frequently in New York City. It all seemed glamorous and certainly the kind of thing she wanted to be attached to.

Already, she'd imagined herself helping Chris host whoever he needed to "schmooze" for a night. They would pour wine and laugh and tell anecdotes, and every single client who left their place would say, "Gosh, what a successful and beautiful couple they are," or, "They're really going to have the most beautiful children, aren't they?" or, "One day, those two will be a force to reckon with."

She just knew it.

Amanda turned on a favorite playlist of hers and danced around the kitchen as she cooked Chris's favorite, eggplant parmesan. Just after the oven beeped to say it had preheated, she received another email update from her second cousin, Charlotte Hamner, who worked as a wedding planner and was refining the last elements of Amanda and Chris's wedding.

> CHARLOTTE: I know you cut it close with picking out that dress, but you definitely picked out the right one. Your mom was just showing me a photo. Girl, you are going to be stunning!

> AMANDA: Haha. It took Mom and I forever to find the perfect one. She said it's got the right 'vintage' flair.

> CHARLOTTE: No doubt. How are you feeling about everything? Happy to be back in Newark?

Amanda placed the glass dish in the oven and rubbed her palms together. The Christmas tree glittered beautifully in the living room; her laptop remained open to show her high GPA; her heart felt full, vibrant, and sure of her future.

> AMANDA: I'm lucky to have two homes— one in Newark and the other in the Vineyard.

The eggplant parmesan came out of the oven just minutes before Amanda expected Chris back. This was classic Amanda behavior: she knew how to time things well and always had. Hurriedly, she slipped the garlic bread into the oven and inhaled the glorious smell of it, wafting through the kitchen and out into the living room. It had been a long time since she and Chris had acknowledged that they wanted to incorporate garlic back into their lives. During their first year of dating, Amanda had avoided it like the plague, as she'd wanted to impress Chris. Chris, it turned out, had done the same. All that kissing had been worth it.

Amanda had met Chris during her freshman year at Rutgers. He'd been twenty years old, two years older than her, with this tousled blond hair and broad shoulders that were obviously sculpted in the gym. When he'd flashed a crooked smile her way, she'd known something in the innermost pit of her belly. She had known they were about to change one another's lives for good.

Amanda took the garlic bread out of the oven and positioned two plates on the little island, where they normally ate and sipped wine together and discussed their days. She opened one of the better wine bottles— something from Italy, and poured them both hefty glasses. Then, she checked her phone to see if he'd texted about heading back.

The phone was dark.

Amanda turned her eyes toward the door. She willed it to open. "Come on, Chris. Get home."

She contemplated calling again. It was unkind of his office to hold him so late in the evening, a full hour after he should have left, and especially during that strange in-between after Christmas and before New Year's.

Still, Amanda knew how important Chris's job was to him; he wanted to rise through the ranks, become someone special, and make a great deal of money. He wanted to support her and their future children.

A few minutes late on a random day at the end of December meant nothing.

Right?

Finally, she typed out a text.

> AMANDA: Hey! I just wanted to check in on you. Are you okay out there? Eggplant Parm hot and ready. :)

She sipped her wine and stared at the phone. A minute passed, then another. Hunger shot through her, and she thought long and hard about taking a few bites of her portion. Would Chris care?

It drifted toward seven-thirty. Amanda's nostrils flared.

Something strange and sickly curled itself in the bottom of her stomach.

But instead of calling Chris, she decided to call her mother. If anyone deserved to know the good news about her grades, it was Susan Sheridan. After all, she had given Amanda her wit and smarts.

Chapter Two

"**S**o you want to stay with us for three nights, is that right?" Susan asked. She formed her fingers over the keys as she spoke to a haggard-looking couple at the Sunrise Cove front desk. They were coated in fluffy snow, and the man's glasses had fogged up so much that she couldn't see his eyes.

"Our hotel in Edgartown over-booked, apparently," the woman explained, disgruntled. "I can't believe you have a spare room."

"Just one, I'm afraid," Susan said. "It's on the smaller side, but it has a beautiful view of the Vineyard Sound. I think you'll be happy there."

The man and the woman exchanged glances while Susan finalized their booking.

"We just wanted a nice, quiet few nights on the Vineyard," the man grumbled. "And it's been nothing but that."

"Our taxi got a flat tire on the way over here," the woman said.

Susan shook her head and tried to put on a sad, empathetic

face. "That's awful. Hmm. Why don't you come down to the Bistro after you get settled upstairs? We can suit you up with a bottle of wine— on the house."

This seemed to calm both parties down. Susan passed over the antique key and watched as they trudged toward the staircase. Perhaps a few months ago, she would have carried their bags for them or followed them to the room. Truthfully, though, she didn't have much energy left for the Sunrise Cove these days.

Normally, Natalie or Scott or Wes manned the desk— especially since she'd taken much of the summer and autumn off to go through the scariest moment of her life— fighting off cancer. The chemotherapy had really done a number on her, but she had pulled through with a new lease on life.

However, tonight, Natalie had a family thing, and Scott was off with his son, Kellan, in Boston, and Wes was back at home with a horrible headache. It was up to her to "man" the ship.

She just couldn't help but think back to her previous days as a criminal lawyer. It had been her life's work. She'd always had a frantic case to take care of, a client who really needed her, or some kind of loophole to find in the law. It had always felt like a code, one she had to crack. She had always loved the hunt to find the truth and win her case.

And it wasn't like she didn't feel for these poor people who'd had the flat tire coming over from Edgartown. It was just that, well— they were on vacation, and they still couldn't manage to be happy. Sometimes, even though she'd put so much time and energy and love back into the Sunrise Cove, she couldn't help but think—

Well, it didn't matter, anyway, did it?

"Hey, you!" Christine popped out from the long hallway that led from the bistro. A bottle of wine toiled beneath her arm, and she held two wine glasses up, a suggestion and a demand at once.

Susan rolled her eyes. "I didn't think you were still around to capture me."

"Oh yeah. Zach needed extra hands tonight, and you know me, I can't say no to him," Christine replied, grinning.

"You would think after all your years of saying no to people that you would have managed by now."

"I know? It goes to show practice doesn't make perfect," Christine said with a sneaky smile. She yanked her elbow upward as she poured both of them hefty glasses.

Just as Susan lifted her glass to clink it with Christine's, her phone buzzed in her pocket.

"Shoot. One sec." She slipped the phone out to find her daughter's name reflected back. Her heart performed a tap dance across her diaphragm.

"Amanda!" she cried.

Christine gestured to Susan's wine glass and muttered, "Take a sip after you cheers, or else it's bad luck!"

Susan rolled her eyes and turned away. Still, as she turned, she did take the slightest sip. She didn't need any more bad luck. The year had given them all enough of it already.

Of course, it had come with its fair share of blessings, as well.

"Amanda, honey," Susan beamed. "It's so good to hear your voice."

"Mom, I only just left the Vineyard," Amanda replied, laughing through the line.

"I know. I just hate that I'm not a short drive away anymore, is all."

"And you know how much Jake and Kristen wish you were a short drive away still, as well."

Susan laughed good-naturedly. "The kids were pretty

grown-up at Christmas, didn't you think? Only a few tantrums."

"Don't talk about Kristen and Jake that way," Amanda joked.

Susan bellowed with laughter. "Cody and Samantha are my grandbabies. I can't have my only daughter talking about them like they're animals."

"Although they do sometimes sound like it."

"Oh, darling. When you have babies of your own, you'll understand."

There was a silence on the other end of the line. Susan sipped her wine and turned to find Christine gesturing something wildly to someone on the other end of the long hallway. After she finished her gesture, she burst into laughter, chuckling at something someone had done. Obviously, Christine and Zach were up to their old antics again.

Everyone was filled with the youthfulness of Christmas.

"Amanda? Are you still there?"

"Yes. Sorry, Mom. I got distracted by something."

"That's fine."

"Mom?"

"What's up, honey?" Susan furrowed her brow. She sensed something in her daughter's voice, a kind of hesitation that she hadn't known her daughter to have in quite some time.

"Um. I." Again, she paused. "I just received my grades for the semester."

"Wow! And?"

Both Zach and Christine whirled toward Susan and ogled her. Obviously, her shriek had been the teensiest bit too loud.

"I got a 3.78!" Amanda cried.

"That. Is. Incredible!" Susan gushed. She smacked her thigh and did a little jump.

Across the front desk, both Christine and Zach performed a

similar action, teasing Susan. She shook her head at them ominously, as though to say, *I'll get you guys for this.*

"Well, I'm pretty thrilled and honestly shocked. And every other adjective under the sun," Amanda commented.

"You should be proud of yourself and all you've accomplished. I know it's been a strange year for all of us. But you got through it. And now, you're just a few weeks from your wedding! Amanda, I don't know how you juggle it all so well."

Amanda's laugh sounded almost forced or fake; however, Susan decided to chalk it up to nerves. If something was going on, Susan knew her daughter would tell her.

"Thanks, Mom, but I'm barely above water. At least tonight, it felt like the world gave something back, you know?"

"Oh, I know," Susan replied. "I remember those days from law school."

"But you had it so much worse— raising two kids while going to law school."

"Worse? No. I just had to be very, very delicate about my time and how I used it," Susan corrected. "With all you're planning and good timing, honey, you won't have any trouble at all. You're going to have an amazing future, my dear."

Susan and Amanda hung up after a few more moments. Amanda insisted she had to get back to Chris, as she'd only just prepared dinner and wanted to celebrate. Susan wished her well and asked, "You're still planning on coming over for the Sunrise Cove New Year's Party, aren't you?"

"I wouldn't miss it for the world," her daughter answered. "You know I don't want to miss New Year's with you, especially now that we're escaping this crazy year!"

"You got that right," Susan affirmed.

When she hung up, Christine poured them both a second glass while Zach disappeared into the bistro again. "What's up with our girl?" she asked.

13

"She received stellar grades," Susan beamed. "I don't know how she does it."

Christine's eyes flashed, and she shot her sister a lovely smile. "Of course you do. She's basically you, but an updated version. I know I wasn't around back then, but I have a hunch you received perfect grades every step of the way."

Susan's cheeks warmed as she sipped her wine. "I mean, they weren't perfect, exactly."

Christine chuckled at her words just as the foyer door jangled to reveal Audrey, all bundled up and barely visible beneath a massive yellow hat. The winter coat she wore, she'd actually borrowed from the back of Wes's closet— due to her growing belly that had stretched out too far to allow any other sort of coat to accommodate it. Her cheeks were a bit plump from the pregnancy, but she was glowing and looked so beautiful.

"Audrey! What are you doing here?" Christine cried. Panic was etched across her face as she took a step closer to her niece.

Audrey chuckled as she unzipped the coat and freed her enormous belly. "I got so uncomfortable in that big house. I had to go for a walk. Don't worry— Grandpa is fast asleep, and Mom is still there, writing a story in the kitchen."

"You walked that path by yourself? In the snow? At this hour?" Susan asked.

Both Christine and Audrey rolled their eyes. "Come on, Aunt Susan. This island is super safe."

Susan, who wasn't as much of a daredevil as Christine, Lola, and Audrey, gave a half-shrug and patted the chair beside her. "Want a cup of cocoa or something?"

Audrey dropped into the chair and leaned her head back so that her yellow hat slid off and fell toward her shoulder. Her eyes looked strange and far away. Just before Susan went off to fetch the hot cocoa, she pressed her hand across Audrey's forehead just to check if she had a temperature.

"What are you doing?" Audrey asked with a dry laugh.

"Sorry. I just wanted to make sure you weren't coming down with something," Susan said. Her hand dropped back to her side.

Audrey shrugged again. "Naw. I'm fine. I just had an appointment yesterday. The doctor said we're a-okay, didn't she, Aunt Christine?"

"That's right," Christine replied, smiling ear to ear.

There was a strange silence between the women, then. Susan stepped out from the front desk and considered them— her sister and her niece, who, very soon, would allow Christine to raise her baby so that she could return to college.

There was a whole lot of stuff to unpack in that situation.

But it was all for another time.

Susan hurried down the hallway and busied herself: boiling water, stirring it up with chocolate and sugar, dotting marshmallows at the top. Zach spoke in frantic whispers to one of his busboys, seemingly not wanting to let Susan know just how stressed he was, even now, at around eight in the evening.

"Busy night?" Susan asked, just as she began to retreat from the kitchen.

"You have no idea," Zach replied, wiping a hand with his apron. "Just when I think we're about to calm down, we get another round of people."

As Susan shot out of the kitchen, she made eye contact with Jennifer Conrad, a woman who worked in social media over in Edgartown, whom she had met several times back in the old days. According to Charlotte, she'd paired up Jennifer and Ursula, the celebrity she'd done the wedding for— which had been an enormous account and a great deal of money.

Jennifer immediately knew who she was.

"Hey there!" she called. "Susan. It's so good to see you. I saw you in a few photos from Ursula's wedding. I went through all of them to figure out what was meant for social and what was meant for burning."

Susan laughed good-naturedly. "I hope you burned all the ones of me. My hair at the time..." She shuffled her fingers through her still-very-short hair, which she had grown back in the wake of chemo.

"Oh, stop! You are gorgeous!" Jennifer wouldn't let her point to this as any kind of flaw. She reached forward, gripped Susan's hand, and said, "You know what? I have heard some of the stuff you've gone through this year. And I think you must be one of the strongest women I've ever met in my life."

Chapter Three

Amanda pulled the aluminum foil from its container and splayed it over the eggplant parm. She shoved dire thoughts to the back of her mind as she placed the glass dish delicately in the fridge, beside her cottage cheese and her already-cut vegetables. It was now eight-thirty and still, she'd heard nothing from Chris. Her heart performed backflips through her chest. Even still, he had read all of her text messages, which probably meant that he wasn't dead in a ditch somewhere.

Probably, he had just gotten tied up at work.

Amanda decided to continue through the bottle of wine and slice up some Irish cheddar cheese as a snack. When she reached the couch with her snack and drink, she took a final glance at the laptop, which still showed her GPA for the semester. With a somber sigh, she closed it and settled back against the cushions. All she'd wanted was to celebrate this huge achievement with the man she loved. You know, like other people were allowed to do.

Just after nine, Chris finally called. Amanda drew the

phone to her ear and said, as sweetly as she could (and a bit drunkenly), "Hey, baby. I've been so worried."

"I know," Chris said. "You texted me enough to let me know that."

Amanda's heart dropped like a stone. She shot upright. Her eyes glazed over so that the people on the television screen became blurs.

"Is there something wrong?"

Chris's voice softened almost immediately. "No. Nothing's wrong, really. Sorry. It's just been a long day, and I don't know when I'll manage to get out of this drink situation with a potential client."

Amanda steadied herself. She took a long sip of wine as she mustered the strength to say, "I'm sorry they've trapped you like that."

"It's important for my career, so I guess I'm actually pretty grateful," Chris explained. "I've worked my butt off, and I'm finally getting recognized for it."

Amanda nodded as though Chris could see her. It took a full moment for her to remember that he wasn't there with her.

"Right. Well, I guess I'll head to bed, then. We can talk about everything when you're home. Good luck with your clients."

"Thanks." Chris's voice remained flat.

"And Chris?"

"What's up?"

"Sorry for texting so much."

There was silence at the other end. Amanda cursed herself immediately. She clenched her eyes tight as waves of fear rolled through her. She wasn't the kind of person to say "sorry" about something so trivial. She was the kind of woman who took life by the proverbial horns. *Come on, Amanda. You're supposed to be strong.*

"It's cool," Chris replied. "See you at home."

Amanda performed her bedroom routine after that, just as she always had before. She brushed her teeth, washed her face, and smeared anti-aging creams across her skin, the preventative kind. She was only twenty-two years old, but she was just the sort of woman who liked to be prepared. She remembered long-ago nights when she had perched on her mother's bathroom counter and watched Susan perform similar rituals. Amanda had felt so in love with her mother at the time and so privileged to see this intimate act.

The wine let Amanda off the hook, sleep-wise. She fell into a dreamless arena of darkness and awoke just past seven-thirty with the slightest of hangover headaches. When she rolled over on her side, she discovered handsome Chris, fast asleep, with his hands tucked up beneath his chin as he dove through dreamland. Her heart surged with love— then confusion.

But if they were about to spend happily-ever-after together, she knew she had to learn to take everything in stride. One day led to the next. They were going to be partners for life.

As Amanda brewed the coffee in the kitchen, she received a message from none other than Richard Harris, her father.

> DAD: Hey, honey. Are we still on for coffee at nine?

Amanda's eyes bugged out. She had completely forgotten her coffee date with her father. Hurriedly, she texted, "Yes! See you there," and jumped in the shower. In no time flat, Amanda scrubbed herself clean, dried her hair, donned slick straight-legged jeans and a white sweater, and arrived behind the wheel of her car. As she headed toward the coffee shop, she found herself oddly grateful for this arrangement. Whatever "mood" Chris had been on the phone last night, she wanted nothing of it. Not that morning. Maybe she would avoid it altogether.

Richard Harris stood with his hands tucked deep in an expensive-looking peacoat out in front of the coffee shop.

Amanda turned the engine off and adjusted her dark hair around her shoulders. She hadn't seen her father since a few days before Christmas— when she'd been able to tell that he was saddened that she and Jake had chosen the Vineyard over Newark for the holidays. *What did you expect?* Is what she'd wanted to say to him. He had cheated on her mother; he'd destroyed their family. He had run off with some thirty-one-year-old super-hot woman named Penelope. That wasn't exactly the kind of thing daughters like Amanda were even meant to welcome.

But Amanda also wasn't the kind of daughter to disown her father. She still loved him, despite everything, and he'd done his best to try to build a different kind of relationship between them— one that united them again.

"Hey, sweetheart," her father said as she approached. He wrapped her in an awkward hug, then dropped back to look at her. "Just a few weeks out from the wedding, now. How are you feeling? Bridezilla?"

Amanda rolled her eyes and chuckled. "Fortunately, everything is basically done. I've been able to relax about the wedding for a few weeks. Just have to put myself in that gown and walk down the aisle."

"And if you stumble or anything, your mother and I will make sure to fall along with you," her father stated, trying to set her at ease.

"Wow. That's so kind of you. Thanks," Amanda replied sarcastically, her smile widening. She'd ultimately asked both Susan and Richard to walk her down the aisle, as she hadn't felt comfortable with any other arrangement. They had both said yes, and she hadn't been sure why she'd ever doubted it. After all, they were Richard Harris and Susan Sheridan. They put their children above everything.

Inside the coffee shop, Richard bought them lattes and led Amanda to the corner booth. The place was vibrant with early-morning post-Christmas traffic, and they had to speak a bit louder than normal to hear one another properly.

"What's new?" her dad asked her. "How was the Vineyard?"

"It was beautiful," Amanda affirmed. "That place is like heaven on earth and so magical at Christmastime."

Richard nodded, seemingly disgruntled. "Although the way your mom talked about it over the years, it wasn't so heavenly. Not to grow up there."

Amanda gave a slight shrug. "I think with everything that happened when she was seventeen, she had to get out and find herself— find her own life. She seems happier than ever now. And you know how much I've fallen in love with Aunt Lola and Aunt Christine."

Richard took a long sip of his coffee. "I have to admit. I always wanted to know her sisters. She talked about them over the years, here and there. I could tell there was a lot of love there. I never thought they'd find a way back to one another. I guess it's proof that life doesn't go as planned. Ever."

Amanda chuckled, as though she understood— but no, not her. She was list-oriented. She had a goal and a vision, and she would execute it efficiently like she did everything else in her life, exactly as planned. It was as sure as the sun and the moon and the stars.

Strangely, her father fell silent after his statement. His eyes grew hazy. He peered down at his hands, thoughtful as his brow furrowed.

Amanda decided this was the perfect time to tell him.

"By the way, Dad. I got my grades for the semester. 3.78 GPA."

Her father's eyes flickered back up to hers. His face settled into a smile that displayed how proud he was. "You're telling me my daughter's a genius?"

Amanda blushed and fell into giggles, ones that reminded

her of long-ago mornings spent with her father back in the house they had all shared.

"Not quite. But I guess I survived my first semester of law school. Not bad, huh?"

"Not bad at all." He lifted his latte toward her, and she clinked her cup. "That's my girl— my brilliant girl. I'm so proud of you, darling."

After coffee, Richard said that Amanda had a few letters to retrieve back at "the old estate."

"If you want to drive back over there, I can grab them for you. I should have brought them with me, but they slipped my mind," he told her.

Amanda followed her father's lead back to the old house. As she parked in the driveway, a flurry of memories swept over her. She could practically see it all: at age four, running head-long across the grass in a princess outfit while her brother, Jake, was dressed as Spiderman and hollering toward a beautiful blue New Jersey sky. Back then, Amanda had felt their family was a singular unit of strength.

Now, a woman named Penelope lived there.

Her father led her into the foyer, where a photo remained of her and Jake, age seventeen and fourteen— Jake in awkward braces and Amanda with acne on her cheek.

"We really need to update that photo," she informed him, slipping off her coat.

Richard seemed not to notice. "What's that?"

"Who's there?" Penelope's voice rang out from the back room, the kitchen.

Amanda's shoulders quaked with sudden awkwardness and sadness. Although she knew her mother was happier than ever, she hadn't yet seen her "mother's kitchen" in the hands of this woman she hardly knew. She wasn't sure she could handle the image.

Even still, she forced her right foot forward, then her left.

She padded down the familiar hallway, past the dining room. She felt like a ghost in her childhood home, as though all her memories of the past had created this current persona— her, age twenty-two, acknowledging that you could never go back to where you came from. Not like this.

Penelope stood in the kitchen. Her fingers pressed against the counter tile that Susan Sheridan Harris had picked out herself as she peered down at a massive cookbook. Her eyes flicked up to find them, both father and daughter. She didn't smile as she said, "Amanda. Good to see you. Merry Christmas." Immediately after, her lips were pressed into a straight line. *How fitting,* Amanda thought to herself.

Amanda was grateful that she didn't bother to step around the counter and hug her. They were only nine years apart in age. It felt like they were in a kind of forever dispute. My god, what was her father thinking when he left her mother for this woman?

Amanda's father ran his fingers through his hair and blinked at his new girlfriend. He then turned his eyes toward Amanda. Amanda's stomach clenched. What the heck was going on? Why was the air so sour? The tension was so thick she could have sliced right through it.

"Merry Christmas to you as well. We just finished coffee," Amanda finally said, trying to ease the awkwardness in the room.

"I know." Penelope rolled her eyes slightly.

"And Dad said he has my mail."

Penelope let out a terrible laugh. "Is that what he said?"

Again, Amanda sensed she'd said something wrong. "Yes, it is. I'm sorry, but am I missing something?" she asked as she stole a glance at her father and then back at Penelope.

"Penelope, don't," Richard tried.

"Because we don't have any mail for you here," Penelope retorted. "All we have is— hmm." She paused, tapping a nail on her lip before beginning again. "I guess all we have here is your father's girlfriend, who is being forced to announce the big news. That's why you brought her here, right, Richard? You weren't man enough to tell her yourself."

Amanda stopped breathing. Her eyes raced between Penelope and her father. She crossed her arms and waited for the ax to fall. She could feel it, hovering above them.

"I'm pregnant," Penelope blurted out finally. "There, Richard. Are you happy now? I did it for you."

Chapter Four

The following morning, Amanda flung a suitcase on the mattress she shared with Chris and assessed her closet with her hands on her hips. In the living room, Chris's football game blared on the screen. It was a collection of squawks and bright horns. Chris had stationed himself on the couch with a bag of chips and a bottle of beer. He was in his happy place, and he would remain there. Just an hour before, he'd explained to Amanda that he wouldn't make it to the Vineyard for New Year's Eve as he had meant to. There was just too much work to be done.

Disappointed wasn't the word for it. Amanda wasn't sure exactly how to decipher what she felt. Slowly, she grabbed various sweaters and dresses from the closet, folded them nicely, and checked things off of her to-pack list. Besides the list of clothes and toiletries she'd packed for herself, she had listed various items she'd wanted to pack for Chris. Now, she scratched out that list and tried to tell herself it didn't matter. He couldn't come, and it was out of her control.

At a commercial break, Chris headed up to the kitchen area

to grab another beer from the fridge. He hovered outside the bedroom door for a moment. Amanda could feel his eyes on her, even as she faced the closet.

"How's it going?" he finally asked.

Amanda gave a half-shrug. "Fine, I guess. I'm almost done."

"You shouldn't have even unpacked after Christmas. You're always back and forth, back and forth."

Amanda turned. She wanted to check his face, see if there was any sign of a smile. But no, it seemed that he meant it all seriously and wanted to hurt her.

"Well, I can't miss the Sunrise Cove New Year's Party," Amanda replied. "Mom's brought that place back to its former glory. She needs me there."

Chris arched a single eyebrow. "Does she need you? Or do you just want to run away from Newark?"

Amanda tried to laugh. Really, she tried. But the laugh rang out, strange and false, and she regretted it immediately. "You know I love Newark. I love Rutgers. I love you, I love my dad... I just, you know. I have to be there for my mom. She's been through hell and back this year. I want to help her through to the next one. You of all people, I thought, would understand that."

Chris turned as he cracked open his new bottle of beer. He stood with his nose toward the far wall, as though he couldn't bear to face her. Amanda realized, at this moment, that she hadn't yet told him about her grades for the semester or about her father's girlfriend's pregnancy. It had seemed clear that he didn't care at all, not about anything except this dumb football game and whatever went on at work.

"What are your plans for New Year's?" Amanda finally asked. She took to the suitcase and began to yank at the zipper, as though just latching up the thing would fix whatever problems stirred in her heart.

"Not sure. I think we have to take those clients out." Chris faltered slightly. His eyes seemed to turn toward the game as the commercial break filtered out. "I'm sure it'll be boring. Just drinks and business talk as usual."

"But it's all for the future, right, so it's good," Amanda said, feeling unsure of her own words.

"Something like that," Chris affirmed. "Sure."

Hours later, Amanda found herself again on the ferry as it dragged her toward Martha's Vineyard. She grabbed a cup of mulled wine from the stall in the belly of the ferry and blinked out across the Vineyard Sound. She had a horrible sense of dread in the pit of her belly. If she'd been asked at gunpoint, what it was she dreaded, she doubted that she would have been able to answer. It was just one of those awful feelings.

When Chris had first asked Amanda to marry him, he had told her that he couldn't imagine sharing the secrets of his heart with anyone else. He'd told her that she was the only woman for him and that she was the only one he ever trusted in the world. He'd told her how much she mattered to him. He'd told her.

To Amanda's surprise, when she walked off the ferry with her suitcase in hand, she discovered Audrey, her beautiful and terribly pregnant cousin, stationed on the dock. Her mittens were on either side of her rotund stomach, and her eyes glittered with the late-afternoon sun. In nearly every way, Audrey looked like Amanda's sister— even a twin, some said. When the two girls had first met on the ferry, of all places, months before, they hadn't been able to shut up about it.

"There she is!" Audrey called out, beaming from ear to ear. "My brilliant future lawyer!"

Amanda blushed as she gave her cousin a side-hug, careful not to bump her huge stomach. "I know it's only been a few days, but I have really missed this place."

Audrey giggled. "Everyone's missed you too, of course.

Aunt Susan hasn't been able to shut up about your grades. Grandpa thinks you're the smartest woman in the world, and Aunt Christine already wants you to handle the proceedings when she inevitably murders Zach— that is when she gets too annoyed with him in the kitchen at the Bistro."

"A crime of passion! How exciting," Amanda laughed.

"Oh, yes. Those two love each other to bits. Bits and bits, if you catch my drift," Audrey winked.

Amanda scanned the dock for some sign of her other family members yet found no other familiar Sheridan eyes peering back. "They sent a pregnant woman to pick up a traveler?" she joked.

"Oh, no. Not really. Mom, Aunt Christine, and your mom are at the little wine bar down the road. I told them I wanted to stretch my legs. It's kind of my thing these days. If I sit still for too long, I start to think about, you know, the heavy things in life— childbirth and all that jazz."

After they dropped off Amanda's suitcase at the house, they decided to walk to the bar that the girls were at. Snow fluttered around them and dusted their shoulders as Audrey finally broke the silence.

"It's too bad Chris couldn't make it!"

"Yeah! Work's gotten kind of crazy," Amanda replied. She could feel the false brightness of her own voice. "I'll miss him, but I guess we have the rest of our lives to hang out on New Year's."

Audrey smiled as she drew open the door of the bar. "You have to be the most mature twenty-two-year-old I've ever met."

Once inside, Amanda felt herself thrown into a series of hugs and "You're back!" exclamations. Her mother dragged a chair out for her to sit on, and Aunt Christine poured her a half glass of merlot as she chortled, "You're going to be a bride so soon!" Aunt Lola chimed in, "Sure she is. Look at that perfect skin! That beautiful face! You're going to be the most beautiful bride Martha's Vineyard has ever seen. Ursula has nothing on you."

Amanda felt herself blush as she lifted her glass toward the ceiling and clinked with her mother and her aunts' glasses, along with Audrey's glass of water.

"I see you guys kept the party going as long as you could," Amanda noted after she took a sip.

"We try," Aunt Lola said with a dramatic flip of her hair. "To be honest with you, I've been worried sick because Tommy convinced me to let him go on a little sailing expedition the day after Christmas. He's supposed to be back New Year's Eve, but every time I look out at that dark water, I get the heebie-jeebies."

"But you know Tommy knows his way across the water," Aunt Christine said, trying to assure her sister.

"I know that," Lola replied with a heavy sigh. "I just worry about him now. Maybe it was a stupid thing, falling in love with such a reckless and free-spirited soul."

"But that's what you are," Susan said with a laugh. "I don't see how you two could have avoided each other."

Lola chuckled, seemingly grateful that her eldest sister had said it. "Maybe. I hope you're right."

Susan drew her arm over Amanda's shoulder and tugged her tightly against her. "Thank you for coming back, honey. I'm sure all this back-and-forth is tiring for you. But lucky me! I get to celebrate my daughter's stellar grades with her in person! I mean, come on— nearly a four-point-zero during your first semester of law school? That's insane."

Amanda let her head fall heavily onto her mother's shoulder. She could have kept it there a long, long time. She suddenly felt too exhausted to keep going. Her mother's hand stretched over her hair and stroked it.

"You must be tired," Susan murmured softly so that the others couldn't hear.

"I am. So tired," Amanda whispered.

After another drink, Susan called Scott, who'd been assigned to drive them all back to the Sheridan house after their early-evening wine trip. When they reached the cozy interior, Amanda collected herself in a little armchair and turned out toward the Vineyard Sound. Directly beside the armchair, as though she hadn't been gone a day, was a stack of wedding magazines, the very ones she'd gone through, night after night, while her mother had battled cancer in that very house.

How strange. She had made so many of her wedding choices right there in that chair. She'd ached over her mother's health and stayed up long nights and gossiped with Audrey and made list after list so that she didn't forget a thing.

As she sat, curled up, the three Sheridan girls popped open another bottle of wine. Audrey dropped back on the couch and groaned with her hands on her stomach. Aunt Kerry, who'd apparently been there to make sure everything went okay with Grandpa Wes, agreed to stay for a brief drink before she asked Trevor to come pick her up.

"He's over there with Andy and Beth and Beth's boy, Will, again," Kerry said with a funny smile. "Everyone has really taken to Beth's son. He's on the spectrum, and he says the darndest things, but there is such goodness to him. He makes you remember that there is a whole lot of love in this world if you know how to accept it."

Amanda had met her second cousin, Andrew, only briefly over the holidays. Apparently, he had been away from the Vineyard since age eighteen, then had fought overseas for several years, and had only returned because Uncle Trevor had been in a bad car accident. Susan had seemed mesmerized by his return and had said to Amanda, "There is so much pain between the Sheridan and Montgomery families. I don't know how any of us see our way through it. But we do. That's pretty incredible to me."

As the conversation surrounding the Montgomery family bubbled on, Audrey dropped her feet to the side of the couch and turned her eyes toward Amanda. Amanda couldn't help but smile.

"What's up?" she asked.

Audrey shrugged. "Can I tempt you with a Christmas cookie?"

"Of course," Amanda replied, smiling. "I wouldn't have come all this way if I thought I would go a full day without a Christmas cookie."

Audrey wobbled her way toward the kitchen, piled a few cookies on a platter, and then returned. She placed the cookie plate between them and then dropped a pillow on the ground to sit on. Amanda pulled herself down from the chair and crossed her legs. Together, they nibbled and listened to the older generation gossip and swap stories.

"Mom's been staying at Tommy's mostly," Audrey said. "And Aunt Susan at Scott's, and Christine at Zach's."

"Wow. Does that mean it's just you, me, and Grandpa?" Amanda asked.

Audrey shrugged. "I think so. I like the days when it's just the two of us sometimes. He is really quiet these days. Maybe he has a lot on his mind. I don't know."

That night, Amanda and Audrey both took to the beds in the two new bedrooms located on the ground floor. Susan decided to remain at the Sheridan house. She explained that she had a number of things to get done at the Sunrise Cove before the big party and wanted to be close by, just in case. In reality, of course, Amanda knew that Susan wanted to stay at the house because she was there. Their time as mother-and-daughter was always way too limited.

She was her best friend in the world.

Chapter Five

S usan awoke early in her childhood bed. It took several blinks for her to recognize it— the posters on the wall still hung long after their stint in the nineties, and the scratchy blankets, which Anna Sheridan herself had picked out. Throughout much of the previous months, she'd spent nights in Scott's bed. She had grown accustomed to the subtle way he shifted beneath the sheets when he awoke and the soft whistling of his occasional snore. God, how her heart grew, day-by-day, for him.

But today was different. Amanda was back, the Sunrise Cove Inn New Year's Eve Party was just a day away, and they marked time toward the end of a year that had changed their lives forever. As she sprung out of bed, Susan couldn't help but compare her health and vitality to even a month before, when she'd still struggled to walk quickly and her strength had bordered on pathetic.

Cancer had come for her, and she'd shown it the door. Now she had a bounce in her step that made her grin with happiness.

Susan washed herself clean in the shower, donned a robe,

and headed downstairs to find Audrey, already upright at the little kitchen table, with a crossword and a cup of tea in front of her. Susan walked toward the coffee maker, which was full of fresh brew.

"Amanda put that on," Audrey said, speaking through the pencil she now chewed. "She was just on the phone with Charlotte."

"Nice." Susan poured herself a big cup of black coffee. "I guess there's still a few things to tie up before the big wedding."

"Sounds like it," Audrey replied without looking up at her aunt. "I caught her diving through those magazines last night like they were about to be burned. I hope she's not having any second thoughts about the way she chose to decorate every-thing because there's no way I'm going through all the stress of November's wedding again. That was crazy."

Susan laughed good-naturedly. It had been chaotic: the Sheridan sisters assisting Charlotte in throwing together the wedding of the century in around three weeks. Susan had still been a bit weak from the chemo and had gotten out of a lot of the grunt work, but Audrey hadn't yet been pregnant enough to get out of a lot of it. Charlotte frequently said that Audrey's garrulous personality and joy had lit a fire under a lot of the people who worked the wedding, including Everett, the photographer, who had decided to stay on Martha's Vineyard much, much longer than his initial plan.

Already, Susan could see it reflected in his eyes: Everett cared deeply for Charlotte. He thought the world of her. And maybe, just maybe, they could fall in love— the kind of love Charlotte deserved after so much pain and heartache.

In a sense, Susan was grateful for her own pain and heartache. Richard hadn't died, of course, like Charlotte's husband had; he still very much existed on this planet (in the very house they'd bought together, in fact, with his new thirty-one-year-old girlfriend). But just because the world hadn't lost him didn't mean that Susan didn't sometimes mourn him. She'd loved him completely for such a long time. And then, one day, there hadn't been love between them anymore.

She'd had to mourn that in her own way.

Amanda reappeared in the kitchen. She clutched her phone with lily-white fingers and blinked at her mother for a moment before she seemed to force a smile.

"Oh hey," she said. "You're up."

"I didn't realize you girls were such early risers," Susan said, glancing at each of them. "I think if I hadn't already had kids at your age, I wouldn't have wanted to get up before eleven or at least noon."

Audrey shrugged as she nibbled on a croissant. "To be honest, this baby doesn't let me do much of anything. It feels like I have to pee all the time and my back... Well, I'll save that for another day."

Susan chuckled, then glanced at her daughter. "How was Charlotte? Everything okay with the plans?"

Amanda nodded. She sucked in her cheeks, as though she planned to say something dramatic. "She said it's all squared away. All we have to do is appear on the day. Pretty easy, huh?"

"The woman knows what she's doing," Audrey affirmed.

Amanda's eyes seemed strange, hollow. Ever since last night, Susan had noticed something about Amanda, something that didn't add up. Obviously, she knew that marriage was an enormous ordeal for her, that she probably found herself in a flurry of emotions and fears. But Amanda had always known exactly what to do. She'd always had a list.

Chris was just another part of that list to check off.

And Susan knew Amanda would do it, and do it well.

"Too bad Chris can't be here for New Year's," Susan sighed. She sipped her coffee, careful to watch Amanda's face for clues on her mood.

Amanda didn't give anything away. "I know. He just works so hard. It's for me, for us, for our future family, and I know that. And there will be so many more New Year's."

"That's right, honey," Susan smiled, trying to reassure her daughter. "Your dad and I hardly stayed up for the last few that we spent together, as pathetic as that sounds. I guess we just got so bored with each other that we wanted the lights to go out on another year."

"And now, with Scott, you want to stay up allll niiiight looonng," Audrey sang from the table.

Amanda scrunched her nose. "Gross," she said, teasing.

* * *

Susan convinced Amanda to head to the Sunrise Cove with her that morning to help with last-second obligations before the big event. Amanda agreed in that same bright, happy voice she'd always had, although her eyes told a story of sadness and fatigue. Susan waited downstairs and nibbled on a scone while Amanda hustled upstairs, showered, and prepped for the day.

"Audrey?" Susan murmured in a soft voice.

"Hmm?" Audrey didn't bother to blink up from her crossword.

"Have you noticed anything off about Amanda?"

Audrey considered this. She sipped her juice and tilted her head. "I don't know. I mean, it's probably just wedding nerves, right?"

Susan tapped a finger against her lip. "Right. That's what I thought, too."

"I mean, I, of course, think Chris is a square—"

"Audrey..." Susan said, giving her a stern look.

"But a square in a good way, you know? A nerdy, good-looking dude who will always bring in a lot of money and make Amanda happy," Audrey finished with a feigned smile.

"Right." Susan rolled her eyes. "I mean, I always thought Chris was perfect for Amanda. I met him when Amanda was still a freshman. He seemed like everything a mother wanted for her daughter."

"Yeah! Like a stale piece of bread," Audrey returned.

Susan knew Audrey always liked to poke every situation until it blew up in her face; it was just her way, just as it was Lola's.

"Don't worry, Aunt Susie," Audrey assured her. "I only say those things because I wish I had a guy around like old Chris. My fleeting summer romance resulted in a watermelon belly. But Amanda and I are different. We want different things. I just hope she doesn't get bored ten years from now."

Inwardly, Susan hoped that Chris wouldn't grow bored of Amanda: of her lists, of her assurance that everything would always work out according to plan, and of her perfect cookie-cutter college-boyfriend-law-school-wedding-baby outlook.

"Ready?" Amanda appeared at the bottom of the steps a moment later. She looked sallow, and her cheeks were strangely hollow, as though maybe she hadn't eaten so well recently.

Susan made a mental note to make that girl a sandwich once within the walls of the Sunrise Cove.

Amanda and Susan bundled up in winter clothes and made their way out into the chilly morning. For once, the skies above were glittering blue and propelled no snow toward them. Susan side-eyed her daughter and snuck her hands into her pockets. Apparently, she'd been so worried about Amanda that she'd forgotten gloves.

"How does it feel to be back?" she asked.

"You know I'd love to be here all the time," Amanda admitted. "It already feels like home."

This was exactly what Susan wanted to hear— and exactly not. She wanted Amanda's home to be with Chris, always. She wanted her to have that immense love, no matter what house they chose or what happened in their lives. She wanted Chris to be a late-nineties Richard, a man with his head on straight and his heart in the right place.

How things changed.

When they entered the Sunrise Cove, they dropped their things off in the old office Anna and Wes had once shared and then headed off to the Bistro to say hello to Christine. She appeared from the kitchen in a flurry of flour and smiles, and she smeared her hand across her white-powdered forehead and said, "I don't know if I can keep up with all the hungry sweet-tooths of Oak Bluffs."

Christine brought out a little plate of donuts and croissants for Susan and Amanda and sat with them for a while before returning to work. "Zach has been hard at work on the menu for the party," she said. "And it's perfect, as usual. I swear, that guy could work anywhere. New York. Paris. He would blend in with all the other chefs. But we have him here! It's amazing to me. When we have the baby, I know he'll have to calm down a little bit and maybe even ask for extra help, but..."

She stalled for a second and dropped her eyes to the ground. "The baby. Ugh. It's so much to think about, isn't it? Right now, it's just kind of crazy how big Audrey is. We tease each other all the time. But soon, that belly will become a reality for both of us. It keeps me up at night."

Immediately, Christine righted her face and prepared a smile. "That said, keeping me up at night isn't the worst thing in the world. After all, I have to be here at the crack of dawn."

Both Amanda and Susan chuckled good-naturedly as Zach appeared in the doorway alongside his busboy, an older teen named Ronnie. They spoke earnestly about the upcoming party and Ronnie's ability to both "bus" and "serve."

"It'll be tricky, my man, but I really think you got this," Zach said, as he delivered a half-nod of greeting to the girls.

"You have to stay focused. I don't want any more of these freak-outs."

"No more freak-outs," Ronnie affirmed with a funny, nervous lisp. "You got it, boss."

Suddenly, the door to the Bistro burst open to reveal Tommy and Scott, both bundled up. Susan's heart jumped into her throat at the sight of them— Lola's love and her own had become fast, very close friends. She stood and shot toward them and found herself wrapped in the cold arms of Scott. Despite the chill, she burrowed into him. Goodness, how she had missed him in the night.

"What were you boys doing out there?" Susan asked as she smiled up at Scott. "And Tommy, I thought you were still off on some expedition."

Tommy and Scott exchanged glances. Susan swatted Scott and said, "No secrets, mister!"

They chuckled as Scott shrugged and said, "Well, baby, you wanted fireworks? You're getting fireworks."

Susan yelped with excitement and threw her own arms around Scott this time. It had been a faraway dream— just a thing she had mentioned to Scott once. "What if we had fireworks?" Apparently, he had come through.

"And you, Tommy? Lola was worried you wouldn't make it back."

Tommy blushed— proof, yet again that he was nothing but a softie in love. "I couldn't stay away for so long. Not when Lola can hardly make toast without burning it."

Lola was no cook like Susan or Christine -- another side-effect of their mother's death, which had happened when Lola had been no more than eleven. Susan's quick dash off the island after that probably had something to do with it, too. No matter how much time passed, Susan still struggled to fight the guilt she felt surrounding all of that.

But time healed all wounds, didn't it? Eventually.

Suddenly, another figure whipped in through the front door. She leaped up onto Tommy's shoulders, and Tommy whirled her around and around, making that same figure shriek, with her head back and her long hair billowing around.

Lola.

Of course, the wild and iconic Lola.

Susan's heart swelled with love and, admittedly, a touch of jealousy. My God, how she missed her own hair!

"Hey, big sis!" Lola chirped as she dropped to the ground and hugged Susan. "The boys really figured this out, didn't they? I had my doubts, but it looks like your party is going to be something special this year. I can't wait."

"Neither can I," Susan agreed. Again, she held Scott's eyes for a long time.

She would never understand why she deserved all this love.

Chapter Six

Ten o'clock on New Year's Eve, Susan bubbled with champagne as she gazed out across the gorgeous crowd, which had crammed inside the Bistro for the festivities. Everyone who was everyone was there. In the corner, Charlotte lifted her chin to whisper something into her new love, Everett's ear. Susan watched as he gave an appreciative, ever-handsome laugh in return and then placed a kiss on her lips. Beside them, Claire and her husband, Russell, stood and across from them, their twin daughters, Gail and Abby, nibbled cheese and crackers and joked conspiratorially, in only the way fifteen-year-old girls can manage. Beside them sat Charlotte's daughter, Rachel, who was thick as thieves with Gail and Abby and often mistaken as the "third triplet."

Just beyond, Uncle Trevor and his brother-in-law, Wes, stood side-by-side— both sipping water, as it had been a tremendously terrifying health year for both of them. Even still, their smiles were electric. As Susan snuck closer to them, she caught them both trying to one-up the other with silly jokes, ones that old men liked to swap. It made her heart ache to know how much the two of them liked each other, as they'd seen so much of life side-by-side.

Aunt Kerry poured herself a glass of wine near the drink table and made eye contact with Susan. Susan approached to say hello.

"This is some party, Susie," Aunt Kerry commented. "I don't know if I've been to one this large since your mother hosted it here at the Sunrise Cove."

It felt as though a dagger poked the very tip-top of Susan's heart. Still, she smiled through the pain of the memories.

"That was kind of what I wanted to achieve," Susan admitted. "I remember those parties, all of us gathered here and watching the fireworks explode over the Vineyard Sound. It was so beautiful."

"I remember that one year we caught my Steven out with his buddies. They'd gotten rip-roaring drunk and were trying to hide it from us," Aunt Kerry said, with a light laugh and a soft nod toward the now-middle-aged Steven, who stood toward the far end of the room with his wife and son.

"Wow. I think I remember that," Susan said. "Uncle Trevor nearly lost his head."

"True. Although who knows what our Andy might have gotten into, had we still had these parties when he was a teenager," Aunt Kerry said.

Susan's eyes followed Kerry's gaze. There, she found her cousin Andy alongside Beth and her little son, Will. Andy had an arm slung over Beth's shoulder and he seemed in intense conversation with Will, whose brows were tucked low over his eyes.

"They really make a beautiful group, don't they?" Susan breathed.

"That they do," Aunt Kerry affirmed. "Andy and Kelli are staying with us for now until Kelli can get on her feet after the divorce. I'm sure it'll be a long road ahead for her. Mike has never been one for refinement. Although I have to say, and I'm sure you can attest to this— it is so wonderful to have so many people I love living with us at home."

Susan's heart drummed with sentimentality. "Getting to know my sisters this year after so long was the greatest gift of my life. The fact that I also got Scott out of it? I really don't know what to do with all my gratefulness."

Kerry nodded somberly. "All we can do is feel it and never once take it for granted."

Zach appeared in the doorway of the kitchen with a massive tray of light, fancy snacks— things like stuffed mushrooms and squares of various varieties of cheeses and mini meatballs with impressive spices. Both Susan and Aunt Kerry took pieces from the tray as Zach cast them both dark glances.

"I can't even get this out to the table!" he cried.

Both Susan and Kerry fell into fits of giggles as they called out, "We're sorry, Zach! You're just too good at this."

Zach blushed, rolled his eyes, and then immediately had a very-near tumble into Christine, who jumped back just in time. She grinned wildly at him, lifted her hand, and pressed it against his bearded cheek. "Remember when you ruined the cake I made for the twins over the summer?"

Zach's blush turned tomato-red. "Are you saying you've been plotting revenge?"

Christine shrugged and then took a square of cheese from the tray. "I'm just saying you should watch your back, Walters. You never know what might happen."

Aunt Kerry burst into laughter as Christine popped the cheese in her mouth before she sauntered away. "I never know what you Sheridan girls are going to do next."

Toward the fireplace, Susan spotted Amanda and Audrey seated together, cozied up as the flames flickered in front of them. Audrey seemed very focused on whatever it was Amanda now told her, and Amanda's face was nothing if not dire and sad. Susan's heart felt squeezed with confusion. Again, she had the sneaking suspicion that her daughter had kept something from her.

She didn't want to live in that kind of world. She wanted Amanda to know that anything at all she felt or wanted to say, she could say it.

Susan took a slight step toward the girls. But a split-second later, she was side-lined in another conversation between Kelli and Claire, who had a flurry of gossip and a number of jokes. Susan found a good deal of light in Kelli's eyes, something she found impressive after Kelli had gone through so much heartache herself. Obviously, Andy's arrival back to the Vineyard had given her something to cling onto.

Plus, there was something about getting rid of two hundred pounds of jackass. Susan could attest to that. The first morning she had awoken without Richard by her side, she'd felt it: *Oh. Maybe I didn't love him that much anymore, anyway.*

Maybe it had all just been a routine she'd fallen into— no longer a conscious choice but a subconscious ritual.

In any case, her life looked pretty darn different than it had one year before. She had spent New Year's Eve back in Newark with a few girlfriends she hadn't really liked anyway, and she'd drank too much champagne and toasted her "new single life" with a sense of malice and sadness. "You'll find someone else," one of her girlfriends had said with a shrug. "Everyone always does."

But in Susan's mind, she never should have gone out looking for anyone else but Scott.

Just before midnight, Susan felt two muscular arms encircle her from behind. She yelped and spun into Scott's broad chest. She lifted her chin toward his and her eyes felt heavy. "Do you think we can just head off to bed soon?" she asked. "I swear, putting together this party has taken a lot out of me."

"Why don't you come outside with me for a minute?" Scott asked, slowly leading her out the door. "The chilly air will wake you up in no time."

Susan glanced out toward the ominous night, the last one of the year. Her first instinct was to say no, that she wanted to stay in the warmth. But there really was something special about it: the glowing snow that stretched out across the shore, the twinkling stars above, and that jet-black water just beyond. Her heart swelled as Scott led her toward the coat closet. Who was she kidding? She would follow Scott Frampton wherever he wanted to go.

Once outside, Scott led her toward the edge of the dock. It creaked beneath them, and the few remaining boats, tied up on either side, shifted ominously in the dark waters. Scott lifted his chin to gaze up at the stars, and Susan followed suit. Out there in the darkness, they could see almost nothing except those very stars, which made Susan question everything. If someone had told her: "you're seventeen years old and out on the dock with Scott Frampton," she would have believed them.

"We've been through so much over the years, haven't we, Susie?" Scott breathed. His eyes still scanned the heavens.

"That's putting it lightly, isn't it?"

Scott chuckled. Finally, he turned his eyes toward hers, and they glittered with curiosity and love and something else— a secret, maybe.

"You know I've loved you since the moment I saw you, right?"

Susan's heart shattered. "I know. And I've loved you every second, too."

Scott drew his left wrist up toward him and eyed the time. "One minute left of this year. One minute. If you'd told me a year ago that I would be out here on this dock with you, I would have called you a damn liar. But here we are, Susan. And I don't want to live this life with anyone else."

When Richard Harris had proposed to Susan, he'd done it with Jake in his arms as she'd stuffed the car with groceries before a particularly heinous long night of studying for law school. "Why don't we just get married? Could be good for tax reasons," had been his words.

Scott dropped onto one knee, right there on the dock. His large hands cupped hers as he gazed up at her. She had to remind herself to breathe as one of his hands slipped into his coat pocket to produce a small black velvet box. She could feel her heart thud so hard in her chest that she thought it would break free.

Slowly, he opened the box to reveal the most gorgeous, glittering ring— an antique.

"Susan Sheridan. Would you do me the honor of making me the happiest man in the world? Will you marry me?"

Susan's smile was so large that it pained her. At first, she whispered her answer— "Yes, Scott," but then fell into louder and louder exclamations. "Yes! Of course, I'll marry you! I want to spend the rest of my life with you!" Then, a crowd roared back toward the Sunrise Cove. Obviously, everyone else had known this was the plan, and they'd all gathered to watch.

Scott slipped the ring over her finger, kissed her warmly, and cupped her head as the cheers and whistles continued. Suddenly, there was a massive explosion that came from one of the other docks. She broke the kiss to peer out across the water, where, it seemed, Tommy and Lola had stationed themselves with the fireworks. Glittering pinks, purples, greens, and yellows simmered through the night sky— a celebration of all they'd been through and all they would soon become.

"DID YOU SAY YES, OR WHAT?" Lola screamed from the dock.

Susan rolled her eyes and cackled. "DID EVERYONE KNOW THIS WAS GOING TO HAPPEN?"

"OF COURSE WE DID, DUMMY!" Lola returned.

Susan hadn't felt such profound happiness since the births of her babies. She leaned heavily into Scott's arms and watched the fireworks rip out across the waves. Tears rolled down her cheeks and immediately started to freeze. She had to wipe her cheeks clean.

When the air got too frigid and the fireworks ran dry, Tommy, Lola, Scott, and Susan hustled inside, where the music blared and people spoke excitedly and more drinks were poured. Amanda walked up to Susan and threw her arms around her. In her ear, Amanda whispered, "Mom, nobody deserves this happiness more than you do. I hope you know that. Congratulations!"

When Susan leaned back, she cupped her daughter's shoulders and peered into her beautiful eyes. All her life, she'd known Amanda to be stable and solid and fully prepared for every next step. But even in the midst of Susan's own happiness, she felt that same darkness within her daughter's face. All she wanted to do was ask her. All she wanted to do was make sure she was okay.

But seconds later, somebody passed her a glass of champagne. Wes clacked a fork against his glass and produced a speech that seemed to come from a previous version of Wes Sheridan— without any dementia effect.

"We wish you the very best, my beautiful Susan Sheridan," Wes announced over the top of so many beautiful Montgomery and Sheridan heads. "We love you. And we want nothing more than to welcome Scott into the family. Happy New Year, everyone!"

Chapter Seven

Twenty minutes after midnight, Amanda eased herself away from the crowd to check her phone. She was giddy with excitement for her mother's engagement, so grateful that Susan had been given this gift of second-chance love. Still, she couldn't fully escape her innermost fears surrounding her own fiancé and her own pressing engagement.

And when she lifted her phone from her pocket, her heart dropped like a stone.

Chris hadn't called. He hadn't even texted to wish her "Happy New Year."

It was like they were strangers instead of people meant to love and care for one another for the rest of their days.

Amanda was stubborn. She'd always appreciated this about herself, as she'd been unwilling to accept anyone else's opinion of her as fact and chosen always to build her own reality. Now, she lifted the phone to her ear and listened as it rang across the Vineyard Sound, all the way back to Newark.

He had better answer.

"Hey babe. Happy New Year."

His voice was gritty, dark, and unwelcoming. Amanda's nostrils flared. "Happy New Year!" she tried. Her voice was false and bright, such a contrast to his. "How are you doing?"

"Oh, fine. Me and some of the guys from work are out," Chris explained. "A bit hammered to tell you the truth."

Amanda giggled. "Me, too."

There was silence. In the background, there was the thud-thud of whatever speaker system Chris's bar had.

"Guess what?"

"Hmm? What's up?"

"My mom got engaged just now," Amanda said. "I can't believe it. My mom and I are both engaged at the same time. It's like a *Lifetime* movie."

Chris laughed dryly. "Scott's a good guy."

"He really is."

Again, silence. Amanda's tongue felt heavy and parched. She wanted to ask him: *Why are we so off lately? What is going on?* But she didn't want to get into it or start something that wasn't necessary. She didn't want to stare at the problem too long for fear that it would only get bigger as a result.

"Well, anyway. I better get back to the party," Amanda said. "My grandpa keeps giving silly speeches, and I don't want to miss any of them."

"Cool, yeah. I better get back. I'll see you at home in a few days?"

"Yep. I'll text you my plans tomorrow."

"Okay."

Another pause. Finally, Amanda forced herself to say it.

"Chris?"

"Yeah?"

"I love you. Happy New Year."

"I love you, too," Chris replied. "See you soon."

* * *

The ominous conversation stuck to Amanda's psyche like glue over the next day. It was like a cloud over everything, even as she gossiped and laughed with Lola, Audrey, Christine, and her mother over brunch the next day. As she stabbed a fork through a blueberry pancake, her mother asked off-handedly, "And how was Chris's New Year's? I'm sure he hated that he couldn't be here."

"Oh, it was fine. Good," Amanda said dryly. "I talked to him a little after midnight since I was out watching your engagement."

Susan's eyes glittered with joy. "What did he say about you and I being engaged at the same time?"

Uhhh. He didn't seem to care at all.

"He loves it!" Amanda lied. "He thinks it's fantastic."

Susan chuckled. "That's good, isn't it? I don't want to take any of your attention this month, though. It's your turn to get married. It's all you from here on out."

As they finished up brunch, Charlotte arrived with her daughter, Rachel. They drew chairs around the little kitchen table and spoke excitedly about the engagement and about Amanda's upcoming wedding.

"I know I said we were all finished, but I just wanted to square a few more things up with you before you head back to Newark," Charlotte said, catching Amanda's eye. "I don't want you to be nervous at all leading up to your big day. Everything is planned and coordinated."

"I mean, you did just host the wedding of the century," Audrey said with a laugh. "You've proved yourself worthy of any wedding."

Charlotte chuckled. "My gosh, when I think back to November, I have panic attacks. And now, Ursula has been out on these islands for their forever-long honeymoon. I mean, her husband plays in the NBA, and he flies back and forth for games and practices and then meets her back on the islands when he can. It's insane to me. Look at these photos..."

Charlotte pulled up her social media account to show off Ursula and her gorgeous husband: beach-side, drinks in hand, with million-dollar smiles, proof that it really was splendid to be so rich.

"I actually just hooked up an acquaintance, Jennifer Conrad, with their social media account," Charlotte went on. "Ursula was complaining that she didn't want to manage her own social anymore, and Jen was the perfect solution."

"Oh, right. Jennifer Conrad," Lola chimed in. "She's around Christine's age, right?"

"Yep. All those girls are," Charlotte said. "They all ran around Edgartown together."

"When Jennifer's twin, Michelle, drowned, that was such a tragedy," Lola breathed. "It was like *deja vu* after what happened with Mom."

Silence fell over the room. Nobody knew quite what to say.

"Actually, I recently spoke to Jennifer," Christine offered finally. "Her mom had a stroke a few weeks before Christmas, and Jennifer took over the Frosted Delights Bakery alongside her social media business to make sure the bakery survived. She's one of the strongest women I know."

"And the Frosted Delights have pretty ridiculous pastries," Susan said. "I remember going there as a teenager. Scott and I would split like four pastries as a snack, and then I would go to the beach in my bikini." She chuckled, then added, "Those were good times."

"Why don't we go there sometime?" Lola suggested. "Jennifer and her friends support the bistro. I've seen them. We should return the favor."

"Why not later today?" Charlotte asked. "I'd love to check in with her and see how it's gone with Ursula."

A little while later, the girls piled into their vehicles and drove toward the Frosted Delights Bakery on this sleepy yet blue-skied first day of the year. Sunlight sprinkled itself across the thick, rolling snow. Amanda dropped her head back in her mother's car and focused on her breathing. *In, out. In, out. Chris loves you. Everything will be all right.*

They reached the Frosted Delights Bakery and hopped out of their vehicles. It was a picturesque, quaint building in Edgartown and very close to the beach. The place was bustling, stuffed to the gills with Martha's Vineyard's happiest and most sweet-toothed. The smells of gingerbread and sugar cookies wafted through the air. Several people Amanda didn't recognize greeted them and said, "The Sheridan girls are here!" At this, Lola and Susan smiled brightly while Christine grimaced. Charlotte just rolled her eyes and said, "Us Montgomery girls could never compete."

A gorgeous forty-year-old woman with vibrant red hair and a perfect smile greeted them at the counter. "Hey there!" She beamed. "Charlotte, I'm so glad you stopped in! And Christine, Lola, and Susan, gosh, everyone's here."

The woman, Jennifer Conrad, stepped out from behind the counter to hug Charlotte and greet the others properly. "Christine, I'm surprised you aren't stationed at the Bistro on a day like today."

"We're actually closed today," Christine explained. "Zach needs the day off. He's been killing himself. And to be honest, the thought of baking yet another croissant turns my stomach."

Jennifer laughed appreciatively. "I'm still pretty new in the baking business. I think Mom will be able to come back by spring at the earliest, although she's chomping at the bit."

"Of course she is. I can't imagine taking more than a few days off," Christine offered. "It's my life."

Charlotte introduced the other members of their party— Amanda and Audrey and Rachel. Audrey joked that she had to eat double the pastries to account for her "bun in the oven," and

Charlotte said that Amanda was "the Sheridan girl getting married this month."

Jennifer's eyes brightened. "That's right! Amanda, congratulations! Wow. How exciting."

Again, Amanda's stomach flipped over. All these people looked at her like she was this perfect bride. "Yes, it is," she forced herself to say.

Jennifer arranged a large platter of pastries and donuts for them and placed them at the center of a larger table where they could see the view outside. She grinned as they sat and doted on the selection of maple-glazed donuts, chocolate-stuffed eclairs, little mini slices of carrot and lemon cake, and a few too many Christmas cookies. On the wall over them hung a photo that looked to have been taken about twenty years before, maybe more. Jennifer's eyes turned toward it as Susan commented.

"I think I remember those girls running around together so long ago during the summers," she said.

Jennifer chuckled. "It used to hang in the back, but I brought it out here the other day. That's us— the Sisters of Edgartown."

"Wow. You must have been... fifteen?" Susan asked, turning to look at Jennifer.

"Sixteen. Close. Yep."

"There you and Michelle are," Lola said with a sad smile. "You really were the exact duplicate of one another, weren't you? It's uncanny."

Jennifer nodded. "It drove people crazy. We always played pranks. I sent her out on a few dates with my boyfriend, just to try to fool him."

"No! That's crazy," Audrey cried in shock. "I would have loved to do that. Mom, why am I not a twin?"

Lola rolled her eyes. "I know you would have gotten into too much trouble. God himself put a stop to that."

Jennifer laughed good-naturedly, even as her eyes shone with sadness. "Anyway, you girls tell me if you need anything else. I'll head back to help Connie. She'll have my head if I make her work alone too long."

They dove into the pastries after that. They spoke about the wedding, the proposal, and what would lie ahead in the New Year. They also discussed Jennifer as quietly as possible, and Lola mentioned that she was pretty sure she'd gotten divorced in the previous year.

"Wow. We're all going through stuff, aren't we?" Christine murmured with a soft laugh.

"It's the only constant," Lola affirmed.

Back at the Sheridan house, Susan admitted she needed a nap, Lola headed off to find Tommy, and Christine decided to do a yoga video upstairs to clear her head. This left Amanda and Audrey downstairs, both quiet, their gaze directed to the floor. Amanda shivered so much she made the couch shake around them. Audrey's hand traced over hers and clutched it.

"I feel so terribly sad today," Audrey whispered.

It was strange to hear Audrey say that as she was always the first to deliver the perfect joke or keep the conversation lively. Amanda hated to see her this way. But her mood suited it perfectly.

"Me too," she confessed.

Amanda grabbed several blankets from the closet and piled them up over both her and Audrey. For a long time, they were quiet. But when they finally mustered the courage, they exchanged their deepest fears as the sun drifted low on the very first day of the year.

"I don't know if I should be getting married," Amanda whispered.

Audrey gave no indication that she was shocked. Instead, she responded with just, "I don't know if I should give my baby up."

Amanda nodded somberly. "I don't know if Chris really loves me."

And Audrey returned with, "I feel like the worst person in the world for leaving my daughter in pursuit of my selfish career."

"I don't know why I thought getting married to Chris would solve all my problems."

"I don't know what I'll feel watching Christine raise my baby."

"I don't know if I'll be happy in Newark."

"What if my daughter doesn't love me because I leave her behind?"

"What if?"

"What if?"

Their whispered questions echoed as they suddenly both looked at each other. They sat beneath blankets, both frozen in terror about a future they couldn't comprehend. Even still, it felt nice to actually say their fears aloud. It felt nice to look them directly in the face.

Chapter Eight

"How are you doing, bunny?" Susan cupped the phone against her cheek as she tousled her growing locks in the mirror. "Just one more week till the wedding! You must be so excited! I know I am."

Amanda's voice was bright. "I mean, I'm such an anxious mess, but I guess that's what I was always meant to be."

"You're right on time for that," Susan agreed. "But you're always on schedule, aren't you?"

"Very punctual. That's Amanda Harris's motto," Amanda joked over the line.

"How's Chris doing?"

Amanda paused for the briefest of seconds before she answered. "He's great! He's been extremely busy with work, but I know he wants to get everything straightened out with his promotion before we head out on our honeymoon this summer. I'm really proud of him."

"That's great, honey. I'm so glad you've found a partner like that," Susan affirmed.

"Yep. Well. I have to run. Brittany, Piper, and I are off to lunch."

Brittany and Piper were two of Amanda's oldest Newark friends. Susan had practically watched all of them grow up together. Now, Brittany and Piper were Amanda's bridesmaids. Surprising everyone, Amanda had actually asked Audrey to be her maid of honor, even after such a short cousin relationship. They had a friendship that Susan didn't fully understand, but she liked that about it. It made her happy that Lola's daughter and her own had secrets beyond their generation.

Susan had a full day of errands before her. She wanted to stop by at the Sunrise Cove to make sure all was okay on Natalie's end, say hello to Scott as he fixed up a few of the wardrobes in the upper-floor bedrooms at the Sunrise Cove, and maybe grab a quick bite with Christine. After that, she was off to Claire's flower shop to check in on Amanda's wedding order. Amanda would be back to the Vineyard in just a few days, and Susan wanted to make sure all loose ends were tied up.

It was her only daughter's wedding, and both mother and daughter were perfectionists. There was no way this ship would sink.

Susan stepped into the flower shop just after one in the afternoon. The smell was dense, layered with lilies and roses and daffodils. It was difficult to get accustomed to it, as though your lungs had to search for the oxygen beyond the scent.

Claire popped up from behind the counter, holding onto a huge bouquet of lilies. The bouquet was much too large for her, and it made her look on the verge of tipping over. She grinned from behind them and then slowly splayed them across the counter.

"I think the guy who ordered these didn't understand how many he really ordered," she said with a laugh. "A little goes a long way. It's quite a gesture, though, isn't it?"

That moment, the door jingled open to reveal a handsome

man with dark hair. As he swept past Susan, his expensive coat whirled out on either side of him. He looked like New York money.

"Hey there!" Claire said brightly. "I don't suppose you're Derek Thatcher?"

"That's me," the man replied. "And those must be mine as well. Wow. That... is quite a few flowers."

Claire laughed. "I was just saying. You might have bitten off more than you can chew."

"Well, I want to make a statement. I guess this is the way to do it," Derek Thatcher said as he reached for his wallet in his back pocket.

"She certainly won't forget it," Claire stated.

Susan lingered to the side as the handsome man paid and took the massive bouquet in his arms. He nodded toward Susan as he headed out and then began to whistle to himself. Susan was struck by the glow in his eyes. It was clear: this man loved whoever he meant to give these flowers to. He loved her very much.

When the door slumped closed, Claire put her hands on her waist and said, "I guess you're here to check in on your daughter's flowers."

"That's right. Just want to dot my i's and cross my t's, that sort of thing," Susan said.

Claire nodded. "I can show you the arrangements I've been thinking of so far. I have all these photos in the back. Come on." Claire turned on her heel while motioning for Susan to follow her.

Susan curved around the counter and followed Claire into the back belly of the flower shop, which was even denser with floral smells. Mid-way back, they caught sight of Gail and Abby, practicing French braids on one another and gossiping.

"Thanks for all your help, girls," Claire said sarcastically as she cast a bright smile toward Susan. "I get it. They don't want to be florists when they grow up. My dreams of having a family business will probably die in this old place. Not like the Sunrise Cove."

Susan smiled. "We're lucky to still have it."

Although still, she couldn't help but feel that nagging sensation— that she'd never wanted to be an owner of an inn, that she missed her old career. It was something she had to continually shove away in the back of her mind. It wasn't worth the time or energy to think about. Besides, it really was nice that their family business remained in the family.

Claire began to show her the drawings and photographs that had inspired the looks she wanted to build for Amanda's wedding. It was all glorious, Pinterest-approved, and Susan "oohed" and "aahed" everything, so much so that she very nearly forgot what she was doing and lost track of what Claire said.

Suddenly, out of nowhere, as Susan continued to go through the motions of conversation, Claire burst into tears.

Susan straightened up, totally shocked. Had she said something without focusing on it? Had she insulted Claire, or misheard something she'd said, or...

Susan splayed her hand across Claire's shoulder and furrowed her brow. "Claire, what's wrong? Did I say something? I am so sorry if I—"

But Claire just shook her head and scrunched her forehead. "No, no. Of course, you didn't do anything, Susan. No." She turned back toward the corner and grabbed several tissues. Hurriedly, she patted her cheeks and her eyes as Susan continued to stare on, helpless.

She was reminded of months before, when her sisters had looked on, helpless, and she'd toiled in sickness from chemotherapy. How strange it was to be in pain while others looked on. She wouldn't have wished it on anyone.

"Claire, come on," Susan murmured as Claire tried to

brighten her face. She glanced back toward Gail and Abby, who now gathered up their things in backpacks and flipped their braids.

"We're going to head home, Mom!" Abby called. Her voice seemed strained, as though she planned to pretend she didn't know her mother had been crying.

"We'll see you at dinner?" Gail chimed in.

"That's right, babies," Claire said, just before a whimper slid out from her throat. "Walk home safe."

The moment the door clipped shut behind the twins, Susan returned her eyes to Claire's and gave her a look reminiscent of her long-ago "mothering" era, when she'd needed to get information out of Jake or else.

"Come on, Claire. What's going on?"

Claire dropped back on the counter behind her and allowed her legs to hang. "Susan, I really don't know what to do."

Was Russell cheating on her? Was she sick? Had one of the twins done something wrong?

"We do our best to put a sunny exterior over everything," Claire continued. "I mean, especially since my siblings are going through so much right now, too. Kelli and her divorce. Andy and his rekindling his relationship to the island after being at war, for goodness sake. But gosh, this. It really has Russell and I stumped."

Susan spoke in a hesitant, soft voice. "You can tell me. Whatever it is, we can work it out together. Big or small."

Claire nodded. After a final gasp, she started, "You know that Russell is head of the Chamber of Commerce here in Oak Bluffs."

"Yes. Of course."

"Well, he loves his job. He takes it incredibly seriously. He pays attention to all complaints and makes sure to go out of his way for all islanders, no matter what. But recently, I guess, some of the books have been crooked."

"Meaning?"

"Meaning that there's a lot of funds missing. And I mean, a lot. And Russell is normally in charge of all of that. He's been accused of stealing, Susan."

Claire burrowed her face in her hands and let out a long gasp. Susan's heart felt like it was being squeezed. She was reminded of last summer when all signs had pointed toward Scott stealing hefty funds from many vendors across the island.

Now that she knew this version of Scott so much better, she knew, in every cell of her body, that he was incapable of anything like that. At the time, however, there had been a strange twinkling panic— was it really possible that she'd misread his character so much?

"Russell is not a thief," Claire blared with finality. "He puts his life down for this island and for his family. We live a beautiful, modest life. We don't want for anything, but we're not greedy. One of my girlfriends suggested that maybe he stole it and put it away in some account— that he has a girl on the side. But honestly, there have been no signs, Susan. He is home on time every night. He has a few guy friends, but they just drink beer and eat snacks and watch ball games, you know? Nothing sinister. I just get the sense that somebody somewhere has set him up."

Susan felt it: that strange itch in the back of her brain.

It was the same instincts she'd felt during her many, many years as a lawyer.

"Claire. When did all this start?"

Claire shrugged. "I guess the first accusations were made after Thanksgiving. But by then, Dad was in the hospital, and Andy was coming back, and there was so much on my plate here at the flower shop. I couldn't focus on it. Now, they're doing a thorough investigation, and I just— well. As you can see, I've kind of lost it." She gave a dry laugh, even as tears streamed down her face.

"Do you have representation for Russell?" Susan asked. It was a different voice, her lawyer one. She hadn't heard it from her lips in a year, maybe more.

Claire arched her brow. "I don't think that's necessary, do you? As I said, we have nothing to hide."

Susan shook her head. "Unfortunately, these things don't work like that."

"What do you mean?"

"I just mean that if you don't know your way around the system, you can get yourself into a mess. It's important you have a lawyer."

Claire's eyes shimmered. "I don't understand. He didn't do this. I put us on a serious budget last year, just so we could account for Christmas presents for the girls..."

Susan was careful not to say she believed in Russell's innocence. Claire was her cousin; Russell had married in. He seemed like a good guy, a very good father, a big laugher, and a great provider. But she'd long since given up on trusting men. They really did get "side accounts" for "side flings." They really did sell their mortgages to assist their side families. They really did have affairs.

She'd seen it all.

"Let me represent him." Susan looked at her cousin. "I will help you get out of this, Claire. But you have to trust me."

Claire nodded, her eyes glassy and tentative. "I'll talk to Russell about it. But thank you, Susan. Seriously."

"Don't mention it," Susan said, rubbing Claire's shoulder to try to set her at ease.

As Susan gathered her purse and prepared to leave, Claire added, "You know, all these months you've been back, I've seen you as, you know, my beautiful older cousin, Susan. I've seen you as this wonderful mother and kind girlfriend to Scott and

61

also as a remarkable innkeeper at the Sunrise Cove. But gosh. You had a whole other career, didn't you? As a criminal lawyer. I can just imagine you in action, Susan. I'm sure you were a firecracker."

Susan laughed as she lifted her hand toward the door handle. She gave Claire a look of honest delight. "I gave so much of my life to that career. I never meant to turn my back on it."

And maybe, just maybe, it had found a way to return.

Chapter Nine

Amanda blinked into gray light. Her brain remained tucked deep in a dream, even as every muscle in her body leaped up. Her phone blared brightly, an alarm she'd set the evening before in preparation.

Because, oh, yes. Today was her wedding day.

She lay stretched back with her head nestled in the cloud-like pillow. She felt strangely heavy, as though her limbs had no memory of movement. Out in the kitchen at the Sheridan house, she heard someone tap a spoon against a coffee cup, stirring together milk and sugar. After another moment, she heard the voice of her Aunt Lola, speaking brightly.

"I hear the bride's alarm in there!"

"She's probably already awake and going over the seating chart," Audrey returned. "She's our Type A beauty."

Aunt Lola chuckled lightly. But all this talk made Amanda turn off her alarm and wrap herself deeper in bed. All her life, she'd imagined herself on the morning of her wedding day: bright-eyed and alert and ready to charge into the rest of her life.

She hadn't imagined it like this. She had never felt so tired.

It had been a chaotic month. When she'd returned from Martha's Vineyard after the New Year's party, she'd felt heavy with fears and anxieties surrounding the wedding and her future with Chris. To her delight, Chris had greeted her warmly with a home-cooked meal, had rejoiced over the news of her stellar first-semester grades, and had chattered to her excitedly about his promotion, the new clients he'd taken on, and the various members of his family who were going out of their way to attend the wedding (some even from California).

Suddenly, Amanda felt her two-person team was back on track.

Again, Amanda's phone blared. She turned to catch it and blinked at the screen. Her father was calling.

Her voice was groggy. "Hey, Dad."

"Hey, bun," Richard replied. "This is going to sound nuts, but I'm actually out front of your mother's old place."

Amanda shot up from the pillow and straightened her spine. "Oh my gosh. Really?"

Her father chuckled. He didn't sound unkind. "That's right. I had the address in one of your mother's old address books, and I— well. I wanted to come to see where your mother grew up, as crazy as that sounds."

"I don't think that sounds crazy," Amanda said softly. "You've known her more than half your life."

When her father didn't say anything in response, Amanda quickly said, "Mom's not here, though. She stayed over at Scott's last night since we have a pretty stuffed house."

"Oh. Right." Her father cleared his throat. "Well, lucky for me, I really didn't want to see your mother this morning. I wondered if you wanted to go for a walk with me. The snow is so beautiful, and I read about this area out in Chilmark..."

Amanda bundled up in sweatpants, thick boots, a sweater, another sweater, a winter coat, a scarf, and a hat. She shot out into the kitchen area to find Aunt Lola, Aunt Christine, Audrey, and both of her bridesmaids, Piper and Brittany, seated around the table, drinking coffee and eating flaky, gooey croissants.

"There she is!" Aunt Lola beamed. "The most beautiful bride!"

Amanda blushed. For the first time in her life, she had no idea what to say.

"Would you like some coffee?" Aunt Christine asked. "Croissants? Donuts? Anything at all, it's all for you."

"Where are you off to, anyway?" Audrey asked conspiratorially, her eyebrow arched.

Amanda turned her eyes toward the front door. Why did she want to avoid this cozy time of friendship, family, and baked goods hours before her wedding? Why did she want to be in the chill and cold of the wild cliffs of Chilmark, with the man who'd left her mother behind?

She couldn't answer these questions.

"I just have to run out for a bit," Amanda said. "My dad's here and he's um. Yeah." She bit down on her lower lip as she looked at them.

Aunt Lola and Aunt Christine exchanged glances. Silence fell over the table. Amanda side-stepped toward the door and gave a big wave. "I'll be back soon, though. Save me a croissant. I'll need it."

Before anyone could answer, she whipped outside. She could feel their curiosity and their annoyance all at once. After all, in their eyes, Richard Harris was cruel, the enemy, the kind of guy to avoid on such a beautiful day.

Inside her father's car, which he'd brought over on the ferry, Amanda flung her arms around him and exhaled slowly. There was safety in that hug; there was the memory of long-ago bike accidents and ballerina recitals and Christmas Eves. She'd been so little; he'd been her stronghold— her rock.

"There she is," her father said as the hug broke. "My little girl, all grown up and ready for her wedding."

They drove in silence all the way to the Aquinnah Cliffs Overlook. When Richard parked the car, he stretched his hands over the wheel and said, "I can't believe your mother kept this place from me all these years. It's really something special, isn't it?"

Amanda nodded. "Chris thinks I come over here too often."

Her father snorted. "It sounds to me like you've just juggled a whole lot of chaos between your mother's cancer and law school. If anything, he should be impressed with you."

For a moment, Amanda thought she might burst into tears. She inhaled slowly and peered out across the cliffs at the violent and dark waters just beyond.

"I know I am," her father said then.

There wasn't anything to say after that. They stepped out of the car and latched the doors behind them. Slowly, they stepped through the razor-sharp wind and sidled toward the edge of the cliffs.

"Jake's family is impressive, huh?" her father said as they stared across the water. He shoved his hands deep into his coat pockets. "I saw them at the inn this morning. Those twins, they're a handful."

"That's putting it lightly, pops," Amanda said, trying to tease him.

But his eyes shifted uncomfortably at that. After a pause, he said, "I can't believe I'm about to be a dad all over again. To tell you the truth, it freaks me out. It freaks me out so much that I don't know how to talk about it with anyone. It's all Penelope brings up. She's got a lot of morning sickness— more than your mother ever did, and she seems to be in a lot of pain. I don't know how to give her support. Especially since ..."

He trailed off for a moment. Amanda was oddly grateful to

swirl in someone else's problems for once. It was good not to feel alone in the wayward trials of life.

"I just. I don't know how to say this, Amanda, but I really am sorry for everything. Everything I did. Your mother was nothing but good to me, and I stepped outside of that. I guess you could call me a lot of things. A jerk. An idiot. Just another typical guy. I don't know. I don't think I reckoned with the idea that Penelope might have wanted a family out of it. That she saw me as more than just an escape. If there's one thing I've learned about all of this, it's that there are no real escapes in this life. You have to live with your decisions. And what your decisions have made up for your life."

Amanda's heart dropped like a stone. Slowly, she linked her arm through her father's. "You were a great dad before. You'll be a really great one this time around. I know that."

Richard laughed softly. "It means a lot to hear you say that, bun. Because right now, I feel like I can hardly put one foot in front of the other."

"I hope you can later. You know— when you're walking me down the aisle."

"You mean if I let you walk down that aisle? My girl is all grown up, getting married, and in law school. Amanda, I couldn't be more proud of you if I tried. When friends of mine ask me about you, they are amazed when I tell them what you've been up to."

Amanda felt the immense pressure of his words, as though a rock had just pummeled from outer space and wedged her against the earth. Still, she formed a smile and thanked him.

"How did the rehearsal dinner go last night? I'm sorry we couldn't make it in time," Richard said as they stepped along the edge of the earth and eased toward the frigid beach just beyond.

"It went well! The dinner was impeccable, as usual. Zach

always blows it out of the water. And everyone seemed to have a good time," Amanda said.

Even still, the memory of last night filtered through the cracks in her psyche; throughout much of dinner, Chris hadn't so much as looked at her. His skin had been oddly green. When she'd tried to make eye contact with him, he'd turned his head around to one of his groomsmen, Frank. He'd asked him a question about a basketball game. Amanda had felt like an alien, even at her own rehearsal dinner.

Just wedding jitters. That's all. Everyone got them.

Just before they got into the car, Amanda grabbed her dad's arm and stopped him. When his eyes found hers, she said, "I don't want you to feel regret."

"What do you mean?"

"About the divorce," Amanda explained. "I know it happened for a reason. It all did. We wouldn't be right here on these beautiful cliffs if it weren't for the split-up. Of course, it was painful. I cried for weeks. So did Jake. But we all found our ways through it. We all had a destiny out of it. And yours is, well. It's this baby. It's Penelope. It's a gift."

Her father nodded somberly. "I know you're right, bun. Thank you."

Chapter Ten

"I really shouldn't..." Susan's voice was soft and playful as it circled the dark air. "Really, I have to—"

Oh, but Scott's kisses. They were addictive. She sighed into them and shifted her body against his large, muscular one. What was it she had to get to? Was it gym class? A physics exam? Did she have to go pick up Lola somewhere or help her mother at the Sunrise Cove? What year was it again? Was she a teenager, or --

"Just a little bit longer, baby."

Why did she feel this pressing weight? What was it she had to do? Susan broke the kiss again and opened her eyes to peer up at the dark outline of the man of her dreams.

But no. There was something—

Oh. Right. She was forty-four years old. This was the afternoon of her daughter's wedding. And she and Scott? They'd latched themselves in the closet at the incredible coastline estate... to make out like teenagers.

Idiots.

Susan erupted with laughter as she pressed open the closet door and drew them back into the foyer of the glorious site of her daughter's wedding. She'd already donned her mother-of-the-bride dress, an emerald green floor-length thing that Scott had called "irresistible" about four seconds before he'd snuck her into the closet. Just as they clattered into the foyer, none other than Christine appeared in a beautiful, shimmery blue dress. Immediately, she crossed her arms over her chest, arched her brow, and said, "Any reason you two were hiding away in there?"

Scott stumbled next to Susan. Together, the two of them held the silence for a long time, exchanged glances, and then fumbled into various excuses while grinning ear to ear like two high school kids who had just been caught making out behind the bleachers.

"We were looking for some decorations for the dining hall," Scott explained, trying to hold a straight face.

"And I really, I um, I lost my scarf," Susan affirmed.

Christine clucked her tongue and ruffled her long, beautiful hair. "Well, anyway. I just set up the cake in the kitchen. It looks pretty great, if I do say so myself. Charlotte reports that the bride needs your assistance upstairs."

Susan nodded and adjusted her dress slightly, which had become a bit tousled during her reckless teenage "makeout."

"Thanks, Christine. I appreciate it. And I can't wait to try that cake! That is if I don't fall over with anxiety before then."

Christine turned to head back to the kitchen. "I have to help Zach with a few more of the appetizers. But, oh, Susan. One more thing."

"What's up?"

Christine tapped her chin and gave Susan a funny, wide-eyed look. "You've got lipstick all over your face. Maybe save the make-out sessions for after pictures? Just a thought."

When Christine disappeared again, Susan and Scott made eye contact and immediately burst into wild laughter. Susan swatted him with her left hand and watched the engagement ring catch the light from the foyer's chandelier. "We have to behave," she told him, her voice trying to feign an ominous yet severe tone. "Otherwise, Amanda will have my head for ruining her wedding."

Scott saluted her and replied, "Aye, aye, captain."

* * *

Susan scampered into a bathroom to fix her lipstick before she hustled into the room that had been set up exclusively for the bride, her bridesmaids, the mother-of-the-bride, and her aunts. Within, she found Lola, Amanda, Audrey, Brittany, and Piper in a state of giddiness and endless laughter. Someone had poured champagne into pretty flutes, and Amanda sat regally toward the far end of the room, in front of a round mirror, looking like a queen. Most of her makeup had already been done, all except her lipstick. Brittany finalized the last of her curls, something she'd done for all proms and homecomings and now Amanda's wedding.

"Look at you." Susan beamed at her daughter. Unfortunately, her voice cracked with emotion; there was no controlling it, not now.

In truth, when she looked at Amanda there in her wedding dress, all done up, she was reminded of herself on her wedding day to Richard. She'd been twenty-four; here, Amanda sat, age twenty-two. They really could have been twins, separated by approximately twenty-two years. Susan's heart surged with love and sadness and everything in between.

"Mom." Amanda breathed the word as her lower lip started to quiver ever so slightly. She stood to show her mother the

71

splendor of her dress, low cut and simple and vaguely vintage. The fabric snuck tightly around her hips and upper thighs, then spilled out just the slightest bit— nothing overly dramatic, nothing like Cinderella. That wasn't Amanda's style.

Amanda was nothing if not stylish, chic. Susan might have said the same about herself, such a contrast from Lola and Christine's more bohemian looks.

Susan's hand covered her mouth as she took in the sight of her daughter. She felt the first set of tears start to brim her eyes, but she quickly blinked them away. She finally murmured. "It really is the perfect dress. You look absolutely beautiful, honey."

Behind Amanda, Brittany cupped her chin and said, "It's astonishing, isn't it? It looks even better than it did back at the boutique."

Susan had the funniest flashback to Brittany saying something very similar about Amanda's prom dress, which had been a stunning black low-cut thing, something out of a Bond film. While other students had worn bubblegum ball gowns, Amanda had been uniquely herself.

"Ah! Mandy, I found it." This was Audrey, stretched out on the floor with her huge belly bulged out before her and her hands hustling around a large purse. She lifted a tube of lipstick skyward as her eyes twinkled. "I thought maybe we left it at home."

Amanda breathed a sigh of relief. "Thank goodness," she said. She stepped toward her cousin, collected the lipstick, and then stretched out another hand to help Audrey to her feet.

But Audrey let out an exhausted sigh. "No way. I have to stay down here a few more minutes, I think. I feel about as large as an elephant. Are you sure you want me to be up there with you? I'll probably cast a shadow so big nobody else will be able to see you."

"Don't ask me again!" Amanda said sternly. "I told you. If I have to wheel you down in a wheelbarrow myself, I'll do it."

Audrey rolled her eyes. Slowly, she shifted to the side, placed her elbow on the chair beside her, and eased herself to a standing position.

"You're just too stubborn to ask for help, aren't you?" Amanda teased.

Just then, Christine burst through the door. She delivered a sterling smile to everyone and then revealed a large platter of snacks from the kitchen.

"If there's anything I've learned from working weddings, it's that the girls always forget to eat," Christine stated as she placed the platter on the table nearest the bride. "I don't want anyone to pass out on the dance floor or, worse, at the altar." She gave Amanda a wink.

"Wow, Christine. That was so thoughtful of you," Lola said. "This thoughtfullness thing you've had lately, is that going to stick around? Or is it just a lag from the holidays?"

Christine chuckled and made a motion to mess up Lola's hair. Lola whipped back just in time to miss Christine's hand. Again, Susan was reminded of the long-ago days when she'd had to help her mother keep the younger girls in line.

"You girls! Why can't you behave yourselves?" she said with a laugh.

At this, Christine gave her an ominous look, and Susan knew she'd made a huge misstep.

"Me? Behave?" Christine arched her eyebrow higher and blurted, "I mean, who was it that I just found making out in the foyer closet?"

All eyes turned incredulously toward Susan. Her cheeks burned brighter than the sun. She whipped her hands to her face and closed her eyes. "Oops."

Amanda burst into laughter as Audrey joined her, "Come

on, mother of the bride! Let's keep your clothes on until after the reception."

"Thanks, Christine," Susan said sarcastically. "I really appreciate you throwing me under the bus like that."

"You know I'm always here for you," Christine chuckled with a wink.

"There she is! My thoughtful sisters, at it again," Lola said. She grabbed a slice of expensive-looking cheese, bit into it slowly, and then immediately scrunched her nose. "What is this, Christine? The stinkiest cheese in all of France?"

"Only the best for you," Christine replied as she exited the room, her grin enormous. "Love you."

The girls fell back into their previous routine— some snacking, others too nervous to even take a bite. Susan did nibble a bit on the stinky cheese and found it incredibly wonderful, both nutty and stinky, although nothing she, with her criminal law degree, could have named.

"You should really eat something, Amanda," she said, just as Amanda smeared her lipstick over her lips. "It's true what Christine said. I've seen a lot of brides go down during the reception, and it ain't pretty."

But when Amanda turned toward her, all the blood drained from her cheeks. Suddenly, Susan felt a strange form of dread, very similar to what she'd felt just around New Year's when she'd suspected Amanda wasn't telling her everything. Susan dropped to the chair beside her, placed her elbow on the table, and leaned in. She touched Amanda's hair delicately and tried her very best to say all the words she'd wanted her own mother to say on her wedding day.

Anna Sheridan hadn't been able to make it to Susan Sheridan's wedding. Heck, none of her siblings had been there, nor her father.

But Susan Sheridan had lived a beautiful life, and here she

was: allowed this special day with her beautiful daughter. What a true gift it was.

"Dad and I went for a long walk this morning out in Chilmark," Amanda said softly.

Susan was no longer surprised that conversations about Richard didn't bother her any longer. He felt like a movie character in a film she had only seen parts of.

"How did that go?"

Amanda bowed her head. She looked on the verge of tears. "He told me he was sorry about everything."

Susan's heart drummed strangely. *Shouldn't he also say that to me?* That was her first thought, unfortunately. She couldn't say anything like that to Amanda, though. She didn't want Amanda to think she was selfish, even if she was just the slightest bit.

"He seems like he has a lot of regrets," Amanda breathed.

Susan inhaled slowly. "Just because Richard has a lot of regrets doesn't mean you should think twice about your decision to marry Chris."

Amanda's bright white teeth slipped over her lower lip, something she'd done as a little girl when she'd been nervous. Susan wanted to wrap her arms around her tightly; she wanted to help her to bed and read her a story and tell her everything would be all right.

But in truth, Susan knew that the moment Amanda linked herself legally to Chris, Amanda would step further and further away from that safe and cozy hideaway with her mother.

They would always be friends; they would always be mother-and-daughter.

But in only a few hours, Amanda would be a wife. That would have to come first.

"I know you're scared," Susan said, again highlighting what

she might have wanted her own mother to say to her on that long-ago day, twenty years before. "But you are a strong, compassionate woman, and you make strong, wonderful choices. Even when you were a little girl, I could always trust you to do the right thing. And here you are— doing the right thing, all over again."

A tear slipped down Amanda's cheek. Susan knew she'd said precisely what Amanda needed to hear.

With whispered words, Amanda replied, "Thank you, Mom. I love you so much more than I can say."

Chapter Eleven

There was a knock at the door of the dressing room. Amanda, who had only just freshened up her face from her mother's overly-emotional talk, turned to watch Brittany open it to find none other than her older brother, Jake, standing there all dressed up in his tux, his eyes bright and his voice low. "Can I talk to my sister for a sec?"

"Let me check with the bride," Brittany replied, teasing him. Amanda remembered long-ago days when Brittany had crushed hard on her older brother. Amanda suspected that crush wasn't totally dead, even though Jake had the twins and Kristen.

"Of course, he can have a few seconds with me," Amanda interjected with a vibrant laugh. She lifted her dress slightly off the ground and rushed toward him, grateful to fall into the familiarity of his face.

Hurriedly, they went into the dark corridor. Jake rubbed his palms together like a quarterback preparing for the big day. "How are you doing, little sis?"

Amanda chuckled. "I'm good, Jakey. You?"

Jake nodded. "Really good. I was just with the twins, and one of them almost spit up on me. Gotta say they keep me on my toes."

"They always do."

Jake bowed his head somberly. "I just wanted to come up and say good luck. Marriage is a huge step, but I've never met anyone, not in my entire life, more prepared for something like it than you. You and Chris make a wonderful team. And I love you."

Amanda hugged her brother, grateful for these last words of encouragement. Her most treasured memories from the day thus far surrounded her father, her mother, and her brother. It was all she wanted.

Even as she continued to swirl in fear.

As she gathered herself about a half-hour later for the ceremony itself, Amanda's smile felt so large and ominous that she thought maybe her cheeks would crack. Her girlfriends, aunts, mother, and cousin, Audrey, seemed to look at her with these urgently bright eyes, and Amanda wanted to match their energy.

Truthfully, she felt about as terrified as she ever had in her life.

As she walked down the staircase, just behind Audrey, who kind of had to waddle down, Amanda was reminded of a long-ago time at summer camp when she'd been forced to walk a tightrope about three stories above ground level. She had been latched to a rope that could catch her the minute she fell; still, the entire thing felt so horrible, as though one wrong move might have cast her to the ground. As she inched forward, she imagined broken bones; she imagined her head against the mud and soil below.

Most of all, though, she had feared her failure. She had feared her best friends and relatives saying that she "hadn't been able to do it." "I really thought Amanda could do anything, you know? But then she took that tumble, and there was no going back." "I, for one, was pretty disappointed in Amanda." "Amanda just isn't who I thought she was."

When Amanda, Susan, the bridesmaids, Aunt Lola, Aunt Christine, and Audrey gathered in the foyer, Scott stepped out from the main hall, where the wedding itself was to be held. As he closed the door slowly behind him, his eyes brightened.

"I think almost everyone is here," he whispered to both Susan and Amanda. "A huge crowd, Amanda. I mean, not that I'm surprised. I got to talking to someone who introduced himself as Chris's uncle from out west. Seattle, maybe? Anyway, he actually designs birdhouses."

At this, Susan lifted her finger to Scott's lips and playfully said, "Shhh. Honey, as interested as Amanda is in birdhouse construction, I think this conversation can wait till after the wedding."

Scott fluffed his hair nervously and gave Amanda a funny, big-toothed smile. "Sorry, Amanda. I always say the stupidest stuff when I'm nervous. And heck, I shouldn't even be! It's your big day."

Amanda chuckled at Scott, who was adorably in love with her mother. Her heart felt squeezed with happiness for them both, yet sour with fear for her own life.

It's your big day. It's your big day. It's your big day.

The words echoed back and forth, ear to ear, like a big basketball in her skull.

Charlotte and Claire arrived moments later to check in on them. Claire inspected the enormous bouquet, the beautiful lilies and baby's breath, which cascaded gorgeously toward the ground, as though they naturally grew from Amanda's hands. Claire winked at her and said, "This is one of my best works, I think."

"It's really beautiful," Amanda said. "I can't imagine anything else."

Charlotte gave Amanda a large, beautiful grin as she pressed her headset and whispered something into it. Her brow furrowed just the slightest bit.

"I think we're about ready, Amanda," she told her. "I just have to go check on something real quick. Hang tight. I know, I know. Annoying of me to say."

Charlotte hustled off and left the girls and Scott in the foyer. Audrey rolled her hand over her stomach and scrunched her nose.

"I can't wait to sit and eat everything Zach cooked," Audrey said. "I really feel like it was my true calling tonight."

"Me too," Amanda joked.

Audrey cackled. "Do you think Chris would also stuff some cake into my mouth? It's really not fair that that only happens to the bride."

Amanda reached out and gripped Audrey's elbow. Her smile was soft. "Aud, I want to say something serious, okay?"

Audrey looked like she wanted to do her typical-Audrey stunt and roll her eyes. Finally, she said, "Okay. Say it before I lose my mind."

"I don't know what I would do without you. Okay?"

Audrey dropped her chin to her chest. She heaved a sigh. "I knew you were going to get all sentimental on me."

"I'm allowed. It's my big day."

Audrey's eyes caught Amanda's as they shared the snicker. They hadn't even had to joke about it before then; both of them knew how silly the words "big day" sounded.

Richard appeared in the foyer after that. He looked flustered, and his hair was a bit fluffed up. He grinned broadly at Amanda, dropped to give her a kiss on the cheek, and then said, "You look more beautiful than ever, bun. Love you." He then lifted up to greet both Susan and Scott. Amanda hadn't fully prepared for this— yet here it was, happening.

Richard stuck out his hand and shook Scott's. He was always professional. You had to give him that.

"Good to meet you, man," Richard said. "I'm Richard."

"Scott." Scott's face played out a flurry of emotions, but he held Richard's gaze. "So glad to meet you on this wonderful day."

"Susie, you look wonderful," Richard complimented her. "As ever."

Susan patted her short hair, seemingly nervous for a moment. Amanda's father hadn't seen her since before the chemotherapy.

"It's been quite a year," is all she said. "But I'm glad to still be here."

"Wouldn't have missed this for the world," Richard chimed in.

"Nope. You said it," Susan returned.

Amanda wished she would have eaten a square of cheese or a cracker. She suddenly felt light on her feet. She gripped the staircase railing beside her just as Audrey whipped her head around and muttered, "You look green. Can I get you a glass of water?"

That moment, Charlotte reappeared, coming in from the hall instead of the staircase, where she had disappeared. It was like a strange game in a house of mirrors. *Where will Charlotte appear next?*

But the look on her face told Amanda that this was no game at all.

This was real life.

And it hadn't gone the way Amanda had planned.

A moment later, the door clipped closed, and the music from the quintet that they had hired hummed through the room. Even more of the blood drained from Charlotte's face. She looked like she had seen a ghost.

"Charlotte! Hey! What's up?" Aunt Lola asked. Her voice

was chipper, as though a good attitude could solve this problem.

Charlotte's eyes zeroed in on Amanda's. She held her gaze for a long time.

"Amanda, have you spoken to Chris, by chance?"

Amanda felt her knees pull out beneath her. It took every bit of strength she had to keep herself standing.

"Not since last night," Amanda said. "We said no talking or seeing each other until—" She pointed to the hall, where, she'd assumed, Chris had already stepped out to wait for her to walk down the aisle.

Charlotte shook her head delicately. After a long, horrible silence, she said, "I can't find him. And none of the groomsmen know where he is."

Chapter Twelve

Amanda didn't fully blackout. There were bits and pieces of the next several minutes that she remembered later; like, she remembered Audrey's big eyes as she said, "That idiot. We'll find him. Don't you worry about it, okay? I'm sure he's just out for a walk. Or he forgot his tie in the dressing room. There's probably an explanation."

She also remembered the roar of her father's voice.

"What the heck do you mean you can't find him? Where was he? Let me find him," Richard Harris blared. He was a lawyer; he knew his way around the courtroom; he could intimidate anyone if he wanted it.

"Richard, please. Calm down." This was Susan, who reacted to Amanda's sincere sadness by showing just how out of control she felt.

Amanda knew her mother well enough to know that Susan Sheridan hated being out of control.

"I agree with Richard," Scott said. His voice was much friendlier, the kind of voice you trusted. "I think we just have to find him. See what's going on. We can't jump to any conclusions."

At that moment, Jake burst in from the hall. His eyes were similarly large, fearful. He scanned from his mother to his father to Amanda and then swallowed.

"Have you seen him?" their father blared again.

Jake stepped into the foyer, shutting the door behind him. He shook his head slowly.

"When was the last time?" Richard demanded. "We can't keep the guests waiting like this."

Amanda's heart had slowed to the worst kind of dreadful beat. She staggered back just the slightest bit. Luckily, everyone was fixated on Jake and didn't notice that their bride was hanging by a thread.

Jake shook his head. "I don't know. I was with the twins, and I—"

"Well, I won't have him mess up this wedding," Richard fumed. "Probably just got mixed up. I'll head out and look for him." Richard turned to look at Amanda. Weirdly, he gave her a thumbs up. "We got this, bun. We'll have you down the aisle in no time."

Amanda couldn't speak. She hated that this day had so much power over her. Aunt Lola walked toward her, wrapped her arm around her shoulder, and said, "Let's head back up to the dressing room, okay? No use waiting here."

Amanda knew that, really, it was borderline torture to wait there. The music which the bridesmaids were meant to walk down the aisle to had begun. Slowly, step-by-step, Lola led Amanda up the staircase. Behind her, Susan lifted her dress to make sure that Amanda didn't trip.

Inwardly, Amanda thought, *what does it matter if I trip? What does it matter if I embarrass myself any more than I already have? What does it matter?*

Somehow, Amanda found herself back in the dressing

room. Audrey handed her a small plate of various kinds of cheeses, crackers, and freshly-baked bread. Listlessly, Amanda chewed, expecting to feel some jolt of energy. But still, she felt so strange, as though all her muscles had given out on her.

Outside, a January snowfall had begun to flicker from the soft gray clouds above. Brittany burst into the room with several bottles of wine, which she said Aunt Christine had given her. Behind her, Piper brought several wine glasses. As she entered, she proudly proclaimed, "I only broke one, all the way up from the kitchen! Pretty good, right?"

Amanda gave Piper a crooked smile as she handed her a glass for her wine. Brittany poured her the first glass of red, to which Amanda said, "No, Brittany! My teeth! I still have to walk down the aisle— and the pictures!"

At this, Brittany and Piper exchanged worried glances. Somewhere in the back of Amanda's mind, something broke. She recognized, in their faces, that there would be no walk down the aisle. Wherever he was, Chris was gone. He was gone for good.

Amanda gulped down a glass of white wine while her friends, Audrey, and Aunt Lola tried to make up a conversation. Amanda watched the snowfall and hardly listened. She knew they said whatever they said to make Amanda think everything was okay, and she knew that deep down, with each passing minute, everything was less and less okay.

Occasionally, her mother or her father or her brother stopped by the dressing room to check in on her. Their cheeks were bright red with cold, as though they'd actually thought Chris had wandered out into the snow. When Charlotte arrived at some point, she said, "Ursula's wedding was almost canceled, remember? I found her out by the Joseph Sylvia. She looked insane. I had to drag her back in and re-do her makeup."

Audrey tittered nervously. She lifted herself from the chair and walked toward Amanda, where she leaned heavily against the table where Amanda's makeup items remained.

Under her breath, Amanda lamented, "I have never felt like such an idiot. Ever. And now I'm being stood up on my wedding day."

"Okay, that's it," Audrey stated. She snapped her finger toward the red wine bottle nearest to Brittany and commanded, "Pass that over, please. The bride deserves to get ripped."

Amanda looked at Audrey and burst out laughing. She hadn't laughed this hard, in a way that made her heart feel on the verge of bursting, in what felt like years. She laughed so hard that a small button popped off the back of her wedding dress and fell onto the floor. This made her laugh even more. Brittany and Piper looked at her as though they'd never seen this version of Amanda before in their lives.

Amanda had never seen this version of herself, either.

She felt absolutely crazy.

Audrey poured her the glass of red and joined her laughter. "That's right. I know what you're picturing. We have him tied up to a tree while we poke and prod him with sticks until he starts crying like a little girl."

"That's... an idea, Audrey," Aunt Lola said, grinning wildly. "I can just see it now."

"I think Amanda likes it," Audrey added, stealing a glance at the supposed bride-to-be.

But Amanda couldn't stop laughing long enough to say whether she liked it or she didn't. She finally forced herself to sip the very top of the liquid before her, and then she closed her eyes as the harsh taste floated across her tongue.

Two hours after Chris's dramatic disappearance, Susan arrived back in the dressing room again and smacked her hands on her thighs. She looked like she'd been crying. Her eyes found Amanda's, then turned toward the glass of wine in her hand. Susan shrugged, poured herself a glass as well, and then fell in a cozy chair opposite Amanda.

Amanda didn't have to ask. Obviously, Chris was nowhere to be found. Susan nodded toward Brittany's phone, which Brittany had set to play a number of old songs from their high school days. Brittany and Piper were both tipsy and dancing in their bridesmaid gowns, trying to keep the situation lively.

Finally, Amanda forced herself to ask. "Did everyone leave?"

Susan shook her head slowly. "No."

"But they're not still in the hall waiting for the ceremony to start, are they?"

Susan shook her head again. "No. Your father told them to start the reception. Dinner will be served on time. Heck. We have all this food. Zach created a beautiful menu—"

"And the cake. The one that Christine baked," Audrey added.

"Well, yeah. We have that, too," Susan affirmed.

All eyes turned toward Amanda, as though she could possibly tell them what to do next. She stared at the floor and felt the depth of this nightmare that was now her reality. It was the worst-possible scenario. Hundreds of people had traveled all the way to the Vineyard to watch her marry "the man of her dreams" in a "winter wonderland wedding."

And the groom had dumped her at the altar, basically.

"Okay. Okay. We should go," Amanda finally said. They were some of the first words she'd spoken in several hours, and they even surprised her.

"Baby, are you sure?" Susan asked.

Amanda nodded slowly. "But I don't want to wear this stupid wedding dress any longer. Besides, if we sell it, we can say it was basically never worn. Right?"

There it was: that Amanda-Harris-practicality. For a slim moment, she recognized herself again.

Claire was sent to the Sheridan house to collect another dress for Amanda to change into. She arrived back with a beautiful black, low V-cut gown, one that Aunt Lola announced she'd worn to a gala event in New York the previous summer. "Claire Danes was there," Lola affirmed, as though this was enough of a reason to wear it to the reception of your wedding that hadn't actually happened.

Still, when Amanda slipped it over her slim frame, she recognized it as one of the more beautiful gowns she'd ever donned.

"Thank you, Aunt Lola," she breathed. "It's perfect."

I feel like I'm attending my own funeral.

This was the thought that spun through her head as she stepped out of the dressing room and spun round and round the spiral staircase, down toward the reception hall. Behind her, she heard Audrey and Aunt Lola whispering to one another.

"I don't think she should go to this," Aunt Lola said.

"I don't know. She'll be able to hold it together with us by her side," Audrey replied.

"You're right. She's strong like her mother."

"I swear if Chris shows his face back here again, I'll take him out myself," Audrey growled. "Pregnant or not pregnant. He'll go down."

Amanda smiled inwardly. She really felt like she was watching Noah's Ark take off without her. In minutes, she pressed against the double-wide doors that led to the mansion's reception hall and delivered herself into the beautiful display of a reception that celebrated nothing at all.

From the door, she was grateful to find that everyone seemed in good spirits. The drinks flowed, the appetizers continued to course out from the kitchen, and she even witnessed a smile from Zach as he walked out of the kitchen for a moment. Toward the kitchen, Aunt Christine hovered with a glass of wine in hand. She lifted her finger and mouthed, "Nice dress," then nodded with certainty.

Nobody had really noticed Amanda or that Amanda was really Amanda, the jilted bride. She supposed that was because she'd taken off the dress. She stepped toward Aunt Christine and sidled along her, all shivery and strange. Christine lifted a bottle of wine from the table and refilled Amanda's glass as the other girls from the dressing room entered the reception hall.

"I think it's going to be a damn good party, Amanda," Christine told her. "If there's anything the Sheridan and Montgomery and Harris clans have in common, it's a good party, right?"

Amanda nodded somberly as the other girls joined them toward the corner. Brittany and Piper, who remained in bridesmaid dresses, did ignite a bit of attention. Amanda decided not to care. She instead caught Audrey's eyes and said, "Tell me a joke. Any joke in the world."

Audrey splayed both hands over her pregnant belly and gave Amanda a mischievous smile.

"Any joke?"

"Yes. You have full permission to go off the rails."

"Okay. Here's one. There once was the most beautiful young woman in the world. She thought she had it all."

"I don't think I like how this is starting," Amanda admitted as she sipped even more of her wine.

Audrey continued. "Over time, she realized that she was overweight. Really, really overweight."

"I really don't like how this is going," Amanda continued.

"She had about two hundred pounds— an entire human male, in fact, to lose if she wanted to meet her potential," Audrey continued.

Amanda rolled her eyes. "Was there a joke in there somewhere?"

Audrey furrowed her brow. "You put me on the spot. It was the best I could come up with. It—"

But suddenly, the double-wide doors burst open to reveal Richard, Jake, and two of the groomsmen, who Amanda had known for several years. Behind them came Uncle Trevor himself, who burst over toward Susan, stopped dead, gasped, and gripped his knees.

"Uncle Trevor!" Susan cried. "What's wrong?"

Again, he gasped. "I'm afraid we have an even bigger problem on our hands now. As of about a half-hour ago, nobody has seen your father. He vanished."

Chapter Thirteen

Susan gaped at Uncle Trevor for a long, horrible moment. Already, she felt like the day was in free-fall, as though the ground below would come undone beneath her.

Now, her father with dementia was missing.

Susan's knees knocked together as the reality of the situation really hit her. She thought she might collapse. A strong voice in the back of her head told her that, no— she had to remain strong, for Amanda, for Jake, for her sisters, and now, for her father.

"Okay. He probably wanted to help find Chris. Maybe he got confused and just slipped out. He couldn't have gone far," Susan said. She turned to find Richard beside her, who looked more volatile than she'd seen him in years. "You don't remember the last time you saw my dad, do you?"

Inwardly, Susan thought it was almost funny to ask her ex-husband this, especially since he had only just met her father for the very first time that morning. My, my, how you could know a person so well, for decades of your life, and then discover how little they knew you at all.

Richard shook his head and grunted. "No. And there's no sign of that damn fiancé, either. I don't know what we thought, letting him close to our Amanda."

Susan snapped her finger to her lips and shook her head softly. There couldn't be talk like that; not now that Wes was missing. Not now that Amanda had joined the party in a sleek black gown. Not now. She tilted her head toward Amanda, and Richard's eyes traced toward her. His face fell slightly. He knew he shouldn't have said what he'd said.

But Amanda spoke pointedly. "We have to get our coats and look for Grandpa. I don't care about anything else. He might have gotten confused with all the chaos. Come on. We're wasting time."

Amanda— Susan's bright and beautiful and totally devastated daughter, shot through the crowd and made her way toward the staircase, presumably to grab her coat and a pair of boots from the dressing room. It was time.

Susan kept the information as close as possible, telling Richard that it did them no good to have two hundred individuals scouring Oak Bluffs, Edgartown, and the surrounding woods. "I don't want anyone else to wind up lost," she insisted.

Richard nodded as he tugged a big wool cap over his ears. If Susan wasn't mistaken, she was pretty sure she'd bought that hat for him on sale at a JCPenney, of all places. As he adjusted it, none other than Penelope appeared in the doorway, having walked up from the reception hall. She blushed pink at the sight of Susan.

"Any sign of the groom?" she asked as she crossed and uncrossed her slender arms.

Richard shook his head. He didn't look entirely happy to see her. "We have a bigger problem on our hands, Pen. You okay down there a little while longer?"

Penelope nodded, although her eyes seemed to flash with annoyance. "I'm feeling pretty nauseous, actually. Maybe you could give me the key to the room?"

Nauseous? Susan balked slightly. Penelope gave her a pointed look, one that begged the question: *Was Penelope...*

I mean, was it possible that she was...

Pregnant?

"Good to see you, Susan. I wish it were under better circumstances," Penelope said.

Susan could feel an ironic laugh bubbling up from the depths of her stomach, but she kept it at bay. Ultimately, she had nothing against the girl. Susan was engaged, for heaven's sake. The chips had landed where they had, and she was grateful for it.

But in this strange moment, as Penelope walked past Richard and Susan to find her coat in the foyer closet, Susan and Richard locked eyes. He looked like a wounded animal as his palm traced over the back of his neck. Susan could see it. Penelope was pregnant. Richard was going to be a father all over again.

"I wanted to tell you," Richard said softly.

Susan gave a light shrug. "It's not really my business, is it?"

Richard looked even more wounded. But there wasn't time for any strange dialogue; there wasn't time for apologies. Susan needed to find her father.

A few minutes later, Susan, Scott, Richard, Jake, Amanda, Lola, Christine, Zach, and Tommy burst out the mansion doors and into the haze of whirling snowflakes.

"We have to hurry. It's going to be pitch-black between the trees soon," Tommy stated. He slipped his arm over Lola, then uttered decidedly, "And I think we should make sure we stick in groups. Stay safe out there, everyone. Not the kind of weather we should be out in. That's for sure."

Scott slipped his hand over Susan's gloved one and made

heavy eye contact. His stance was clear: they would go through this together. They struck out toward the closest line of trees as Susan's inner mind screamed with sadness and turmoil. Just before they plunged into the darkness, someone grabbed Susan's upper arm. She nearly leaped out of her coat.

"Hey! Susie." It was Christine, alongside Zach. "We're going to head to Oak Bluffs and check around the house. No telling what might have happened. Maybe he got a ride back home and is fast asleep in bed."

"Good idea," Susan said. "I don't know what to make of any of this." At that moment, she thought she might burst into tears.

Hold it together, Susan. You have to be strong for everyone else.

"We'll be in touch," Zach affirmed. "And we've called the sheriff, just in case."

"Good. Thank you," Susan replied, cursing herself for not taking that obvious action.

Susan and Scott made their way out into the woods, which grew thicker then thinner again as it eased toward the little town on the other side. Susan and Scott called Wes's name as loud as they could, with Susan occasionally yelling, "DAD!" Within minutes, her voice was hoarse and her lips were chapped, but they kept going.

After twenty-five minutes, Susan stopped short, huffed, and leaned against the nearest tree. Through the hazy darkness, she peered at Scott. She wanted to tell him how hopeless she felt.

"I can't believe how this day has gone," she finally said.

Scott shook his head and placed his hands on his hips. He gazed out through the trees. It seemed like, for miles and miles in every direction, they were alone on a rock in the middle of the ocean. It was an alienating feeling.

"None of it is your fault, Susan," he finally said.

But to Susan, the words rang false.

"I should have kept my eye on Dad. Everything ran off the rails, and I was worried about Amanda, and I was listening to Richard prattle on about how much he hated Chris in the first place, and I—"

Scott shook his head in disagreement. "No. Susan. Listen to me." He gripped her shoulders as tears rolled down her cheeks. Above them, the moon had begun to duck out of the top of a cloud. "None of this is your fault, okay? And we're going to find your father. This island isn't so big that we won't be able to find the island-famous Wes Sheridan on it. No doubt, he's just telling a story to someone who doesn't want to hear it."

Susan laughed sadly. "And they're nodding along as though they like it and want to hear more."

"No doubt," Scott said, giving her a tender smile.

They continued to look. Several minutes later, Amanda called. Her voice was bright but strange.

"Jake and I haven't had any luck yet," she said. "What about you guys?"

"Nothing here," Susan said. Her teeth clattered with a chill.

"Okay. I just hadn't heard from anyone and wanted to reach out," Amanda said. "But Mom, it's going to be okay. It has to be."

"Okay, honey." Susan couldn't help but think: *I should be saying this to you, the jilted bride.* But instead, she hung up.

Throughout the search, Susan was reminded of a long-ago day, probably twenty-one years ago, when she'd lost Jake at a grocery store. She'd had Amanda strapped to her front, and she'd only gotten her to sleep after hours of gut-busting baby screams. With a panicked heart, Susan had whipped through the store, taking stock of every toddler, before then analyzing every adult. *Did you take my child? Why did you take my child?*

What do you want with him? Don't you know I will kill you if you hurt him?

Of course, she had ultimately found Jake in front of the live lobster tanks, with his big, fat palms pressed up against the glass. When she'd spotted him, the person behind the counter had said, "I wondered what this little guy was up to. He seemed like he could communicate with them."

Enraged, Susan had wanted to demand why this incompetent worker at the counter hadn't alerted the store of a toddler who stood by himself, clearly alone. Instead, she'd burst into tears, woken up Amanda, and filled all the grocery aisles with the songs of her family's fears and sadness.

She felt like that now, here in the gray woods with Scott.

She felt completely out of control.

A few minutes later, Lola called to say there still hadn't been word. Susan felt the hesitation and fear in her voice. She knew they were running out of time, whatever the heck that meant. An old man like Wes couldn't be out in the cold like this, not for long. Susan's toes ached as snow crept into the bottom of her boots and melted. She cursed herself for not having packed her hiking boots.

Finally, about an hour after Uncle Trevor had first sounded the alarm that Wes was missing, Susan received a call from an unknown number.

"Hello?" Her voice was frantic.

"Susan, hey. It's Walter, you know, from the Main Street Saloon."

Susan's heart hammered wildly in her chest. This was a bar that Wes had spent a good deal of time at over the summer; he'd been a regular throughout much of his adult life on the island.

"Is he there? Have you found him?" Susan blurted.

"He's here," Walter affirmed. He sounded hesitant. "But he's pretty messed up, Susan. He looks like he's been outside for a long time. He...he collapsed the minute he got in here. He doesn't know where he is or how he got here. We've already called the ambulance. I guess you'd better meet him up at the hospital."

Susan dropped her chin to her chest. Through all her confused thoughts, all she could think was: *he's still alive. He's still here. Maybe he'll be all right.*

"Thank you, Walter. Really. I can't tell you how worried we've been."

Susan and Scott hustled back to the mansion. Throughout the whip-fast walk, Susan dialed the others to inform them of what had happened. "I'm headed to the hospital right now," Susan told Christine, then Lola, then Richard, then Amanda.

Amanda, notably, breathed the biggest sigh of relief. "Mom, I am so sorry about today."

Susan stopped short just before she leaped into Scott's truck. She peered at her reflection in Scott's window, suddenly fully aware of the devastation of the day— a day that Amanda had looked forward to since she'd been a little girl.

"Baby, this is not your fault," Susan said, trying to assure her. "Sometimes, everything falls apart. It's something I've had to learn over the past twenty-some years of my life."

And now, it seems like it's time for you to learn it, too.

"I'll see you at the hospital, Mom," Amanda said, her voice breaking. "I love you."

Susan squeezed her eyes closed as she slipped into the front seat and slammed the door closed. "I love you, too," she breathed before she realized Amanda had already hung up the phone. Tears slipped down her cheeks as Scott reached out and gripped her hand.

"I never wanted her to know all the pain I went through," Susan whispered as Scott drove out of the mansion lot and out toward the road that would take them back to the hospital in Oak Bluffs— the very one where she'd reconnected with her father more than six months before.

"All you can do is try to guide her through, the best you know how," Scott told her as his hand slowly warmed her frigid skin. "You can't change it. You can just tell her that one day, she won't feel it quite the same way anymore. It will be a distant memory, nothing more."

Chapter Fourteen

It was now Wednesday. Amanda blinked at the date on the calendar, as though it had betrayed her. But no: time moved on, whether you liked it or not, and here she was, living out the first week she had been meant to be Chris's wife. And still, days after the wedding, she hadn't spoken a single word to her no longer groom-to-be.

Amanda stood alone at the Sheridan house. She wore the same ratty t-shirt she'd donned that Saturday night after she had returned from the hospital; her sweatpants had a wine stain along with a little melted cheese and even some chocolate across the right knee. Her normally gorgeous hair, which she kept up impeccably, had been tied in a messy bun and she no longer knew the blissfulness of a shower.

Is this how I'll live out the rest of my life? A complete and utter mess? Sweatpant-chic? Jilted bride couture?

Amanda sprayed cleaning solution across the counter and began to wipe a washcloth across it. Admittedly, she had already cleaned this counter twice that morning, but she just needed to do something, anything with her hands. After this, she would rearrange the fridge for the fourth time and maybe go through the front closet to see what could be thrown out. But then what? Clean every window in the entire house? That would probably take days. It was perfect. Maybe she could milk it for a full week.

When the doctor had announced that Wes just needed several days of bed rest at the hospital, followed by several weeks of rest back at the Sheridan house, the Sheridan and Montgomery families had breathed a collective sigh of relief and returned to their homes. According to reports from Brittany and Piper, Amanda and Chris's wedding reception had raged on into the night. "It was one of the best parties I've been to in years," is what Brittany had said. Sometimes, Brittany could be tone-deaf; this was one of those cases.

Still, Amanda was glad that some people had enjoyed her wedding.

Apparently, the groomsmen had dug into the glorious wedding cake that Christine had baked for her, smashing one another in the face with it.

Truthfully, Amanda had never really liked Chris's friends.

Maybe this was proof that she and Chris hadn't really been meant to...

No. She wasn't ready to say that yet.

After she hadn't heard anything from Chris on Saturday evening and then into Sunday morning, Amanda had turned off her cell phone and hadn't bothered to turn it back on. This annoyed her mother to no end, but it was her twenty-first-century version of "hiding from the world." This way, she couldn't ogle the Instagram photos people had posted from her "wedding." She couldn't know what Chris was up to. And best of all: nobody could contact her. Not Chris, not her friends, and not anybody who had "words of pity." She didn't have time for it.

All she had time to do, right here and now, was clean every

single square inch of the Sheridan house. Maybe this was her destiny for the time being.

The previous evening, when Lola had caught her cleaning the upstairs bathroom yet again, she'd said, "I've never seen anyone more productive than you, Amanda."

At this, Amanda had joked, "Leave it to me to be the lamest depressed person on the planet. Most other people eat ice cream and watch their favorite movies."

"Ah, well. If you get to that stage, call me. I love ice cream and movies," Aunt Lola had teased. "But first, maybe I should have you over to mine and Tommy's cottage. I love Tommy, but if I stay over here too long, that place looks like a tornado ripped through it."

After Amanda wiped down the counter for the millionth time, her stomach fought with her and demanded at least the tiniest bit of food. It had been a struggle to keep things down, and normally, she felt much too upset to think of anything she might like to eat. Somberly, she placed a slice of cheese on her tongue and forced herself to chew. With every motion of her jaw, her brain played tricks on her.

Chris left you because you're too boring.

Chris left you because you're not pretty enough.

Chris left you because you're too anal about cleaning.

Chris left you because you make too many stupid lists.

Chris left you because—

Even this was another list, Amanda told herself. She chewed the rest of her cheese, swallowed it, and then fell back onto the kitchen floor, where she wrapped herself in a ball.

You don't deserve happiness.

You don't deserve marriage or children or law school or anything you've planned for.

You just deserve this.

Just then, there was the creak of the tires across the driveway. Amanda leaped up, touched her messy bun, and scrunched her nose. All morning, her mother had worked at the Sunrise Cove; after that, she'd planned to bring Wes home. They'd set up one of the downstairs bedrooms for him so that he didn't have to climb the stairs all the time. Audrey had opted to move upstairs.

Amanda opened the door to allow Scott to wheel her grandfather through the back door. Her grandfather grinned up at her, bright-eyed, with a few slice-like cuts across his forehead, maybe from twigs, although it was difficult to say. They assumed that he'd wandered through the woods before he'd stumbled into the saloon, but there was really no telling what had happened. Wes had no memories associated with it.

And in fact, he seemed foggier than ever.

"Hey there," Amanda said, grateful her voice didn't break as her mother, Scott, and Wes positioned themselves around the kitchen table.

Susan lifted a bag of Christine's croissants and wagged her eyebrows. "Christine is on her way, but she sent these along with me this morning so we could have a little welcome-home snack. Dad, what do you think about that?"

Wes still blinked at Amanda, seemingly perplexed. Amanda knew that she looked a great deal like her grandmother, Anna, back when she'd been in her twenties; she and Audrey both did. She dropped her eyes to the ground, praying that her grandfather wouldn't call her Anna. It was something she couldn't emotionally handle.

Finally, he said, "Amanda. There you are." His shaky hands drew out a croissant and began to strip off bits of the flaky goodness.

"Hi, Grandpa!" Amanda smiled. "I'm so glad to have you home."

Wes nodded as he looked at her. Slowly, he took a bite from the croissant. He didn't have much strength; even his muscles looked depleted. Amanda swallowed the lump that had formed in her throat. It was sad to see everything change, even this.

"Amanda, I really am looking forward to your wedding," her grandfather said. A secretive smile snuck across his face. "How privileged I am to be able to watch one of my granddaughters get married, only a few months before another of my granddaughters gives me a great-grandchild. It's a remarkable gift."

Susan's eyes widened in shock while Scott placed his croissant back on his plate and looked at Amanda, panicked.

But there was nothing Amanda could do but laugh.

"That's sweet, Grandpa," she replied. "I will love having you there."

Inwardly, it felt like every single organ, from her heart to her lungs to her brain, was on fire. There was no way she could possibly live through this. Right?

Somehow, in some way, Amanda found herself able to sit with Scott and her mother and her grandfather and have some kind of normal conversation. Her mother eyed her curiously, as though she was a ticking time bomb about to go off. But Amanda found ways to joke and laugh and carry on a conversation until Wes announced he was pretty tired and wanted to lie down for the afternoon. Scott wheeled him into the bedroom, helped him into the bed, and then pulled the door closed behind him. He nodded toward Susan and said, "He looks comfy in there for now. I think he's just glad to be home."

Susan pressed her hand to her chest. "I'm so glad he's here. Oh, but Amanda. I'm so sorry about—"

Amanda waved her hand in the air between them. Hurriedly, she picked up the plates and the trash from the table and began to frantically clean again. Over the scrubbing and the sound of the faucet, she heard Scott tell her mother he wanted to get a few things done at the Sunrise Cove that afternoon. He bent to kiss her goodbye. A few minutes later, he disappeared into the gray light of yet another January day.

The Wednesday after Amanda's wedding.

"Amanda?"

Her mother's voice rang out over the sound of the faucet. Amanda pretended not to hear for a moment.

"Amanda? Can you sit with me for a moment, please?"

She sucked in a breath. Amanda felt like a teenager again, ordered to the dining room table to discuss some problems with her parents. Slowly, she turned the faucet off and dried her hands with a dishcloth. When she turned, she found her mother's face blotchy.

"Just for a sec, Mandy," Susan said as she patted the table-space across from her. "Then you can get back to whatever you want to do."

Whatever the heck you want to clean next was the subtext.

Amanda sat. She crossed and uncrossed her arms over her breasts and prayed to high heaven that she didn't actually reek to high heaven, even though she hadn't bothered with much hygiene. She felt like an exposed nerve, there in front of her mother. Before she knew what hit her, tears began to course down her cheeks.

"I'm sorry, Mom," Amanda cried.

Susan furrowed her brow. "Amanda, no. No, no. You have nothing to be sorry about." She reached across the table, found Amanda's hands, and dragged them out to the center of the beautiful wood. Her thumb traced tenderly over Amanda's palm. "You didn't do anything wrong, okay?"

Amanda closed her eyes and tried to breathe. Finally, she said, "I know you're upset that I've already missed a few days of classes."

Susan chuckled, not unkindly. "No. Of course I'm not upset. Why would I be?"

Amanda shrugged. "I don't know. Because I did so well last semester. And I have all this potential. And—"

"Those sound more like things you're telling yourself," Susan said. "And they sound reasonable. But you just went through one of the hardest things you will ever have to go through in your life. I think you're doing what you have to do to survive it. No pressure on my side, okay? Besides. You're Amanda Harris. I know you know what you need to do. It's your thing."

Amanda bit hard on her lower lip. Slowly, she forced herself to open her eyes. "I just don't know how I can go back to Newark like this. I don't know how I can face my friends, or go back to law school, or even enter that apartment."

Susan's eyes shimmered. She looked vaguely surprised, although she looked like she didn't want to show it.

"I see."

"I already looked it up," Amanda explained hurriedly. "Several of my classes have the option of being online-only if I go to the end-of-semester final in person. A few others, I can push off to other semesters, maybe. I just..." She again bit hard on her lower lip, feeling like a child. "I really think I want to stay here— in this house. I don't trust the rest of the world right now. I need to stay on the Vineyard. I need—"

Just then, the back door screeched open, and Aunt Lola's voice rang out. "Hello! It smells like cleaning supplies in here. Has our little house elf been hard at work again?"

Susan's eyes didn't leave Amanda's for a long moment. Within them, Amanda saw fear and sadness and maybe the tiniest glimmer of disappointment.

After all, Amanda had just told her mother something she'd never told anyone before.

She wanted to give up.

She wanted to hide.

And she didn't know what was next.

Chapter Fifteen

Susan peeked her head into the room beside Wes's, where Amanda remained in the days after being stood up for her own wedding. It was just past seven-thirty in the morning. A normal Amanda, an Amanda of another era, would have been wide awake by now— draped over her computer and typing away, already scribing a list for the morning ahead.

But the Amanda of now was still nestled back in bed, her bun all messy, like a bird's nest atop the pillow. Susan's heart dropped in her stomach. Throughout Amanda's youth and into her teenage years, Amanda had never really gone through a "tough spot." She had always been the number one student, a good and caring friend, a wonderful sister to Jake, and a dream of a daughter.

How strange to find the doldrums now, at age twenty-two. When she had announced that she wanted to take several of her classes online and not return to Newark, Susan had very nearly jumped down her throat. She'd felt the words bubbling in her stomach: *What do you mean? Give up? Because of that idiot, Chris? No. You can't.*

But she'd seen the darkness behind Amanda's eyes. This was the answer, whether Susan liked it or not.

The floor creaked behind her. Susan whirled around to find Audrey in a big, light pink robe, the very one Anna Sheridan had worn before her death. It was overwhelming, all these memories at once. Susan shut Amanda's door closed quietly and whispered, "Good morning," to Audrey.

Audrey smiled sleepily. "I see you're spying on Mandy?"

Susan shrugged. "I'm worried about her. It's not like her to sleep in so much."

"It's only seven-thirty," Audrey said. "Chances are that my own mother won't be awake for another two hours."

"Yeah, well. That's Lola for you. Not Amanda." She gave a sad shrug as Audrey turned toward the kettle and began to brew some tea. "Listen, Audrey. I'm going to head off for the morning."

"You headed to the Sunrise Cove? I thought Natalie had the front desk."

"She does. But I'm actually meeting with Claire and her husband, Russell."

Audrey nodded, bored. "Okay. I'll make sure Grandpa and Amanda get something to eat."

"Thanks, Aud. You're the best," Susan said before slipping toward the front door.

Audrey chuckled. "Not the best. Never the best. Just have to earn my keep around here."

Susan gripped the steering wheel with bright red hands. She drove the familiar route toward Claire's flower shop, where she had agreed to meet with both Russell and Claire regarding the charges against Russell and his apparent "thievery." Susan had analyzed him in greater detail when she'd been able to at the wedding. In her eyes, he was just a loving, kind father and husband, a man who put Martha's Vineyard above all things except his family.

He wasn't the kind of guy to do this.

At least, Susan didn't initially think so. She hadn't gone over all the evidence. She had to put her "mother, daughter, and islander" brain on hold and revert back to her criminal lawyer hat.

"Hey there," she greeted them brightly as she entered to find Claire and Russell hunkered over two cups of coffee. Both looked like they had lost weight due to the stress. Claire had huge bags under her eyes, and her "hello" was sour and strange. This situation had obviously taken a toll on them.

"Thanks so much for coming by," Russell said somberly. He straightened himself and struck his hand out over the counter to shake Susan's hand.

"We have some coffee in the back if you want it?" Claire asked. Again, she looked like a wounded animal.

"Absolutely," Susan said, as though she hadn't hung out at this very flower shop time and time again over the past six months.

A few minutes later, the three of them sat around a little table in the back while Russell described the evidence the prosecutors thought they had against him. "The minute this starts, there's going to be non-stop gossip around it, and I don't know if I'm fully ready for that," he admitted. He placed his face in his hands and heaved a sigh. "All my life, I've avoided scandal. I don't even know how this happened."

"It's just bad luck," Claire insisted. "Or worse. Someone has it out for us."

Susan flipped through the folders Russell passed over, which included information about his years of employment at the Chamber of Commerce, the various purchases he had overseen, that sort of thing. He also showed her the purchases that the prosecutors claimed he had made— none of which he had anything to do with. "I don't know what any of this is about," he proclaimed, pointing to a hot tub and a memory foam mattress and even a speedboat, which cost around $300,000.

It was an exorbitant amount of funds. Susan glanced back up and analyzed Russell, his clothes, his face. He was just an ordinary guy, with ordinary Martha's Vineyard fashion and shoes that seemed much more scuffed than other islanders' shoes.

"I want to thank you both for letting me take this on," Susan said a few minutes later after she'd asked a number of questions and recorded Russell's answers. She shook their hands and nodded firmly. "Remember that before you really knew me as an adult, I was a criminal defense lawyer in Newark for the office of Harris and Harris. You can Google it; my picture still comes up. We had an excellent track record. I'm sure if you called my ex-husband, he would give you a stellar recommendation—"

Claire and Russell waved their hands. "No, no," Claire interjected. "That's unnecessary. We know you, Susan. We're just surprised, with all you have to do, and all you have to take care of, that you even want to take us on."

Something in the back of Susan's mind began to burn. It was true what they said; she had a lot on her plate. Still, she grinned through the pain.

"I do what I love," she replied with renewed vigor. "I just wish there were more hours in a day."

* * *

Susan drove over to the Sunrise Cove to check in on Natalie, who was just as bright and happy as ever. She greeted Susan with a hug and told her about the rooms she had booked, both over the phone and online. "Looks like we've surpassed our previous January booking by two-hundred percent!" she announced. "You should really tell your dad when you get home. He always loved that number stuff."

"I will, Nat. Thanks."

"How is he doing, by the way?" Natalie asked. A little wrinkle formed between her eyebrows.

Susan thought back to the previous night when he'd stared listlessly at his clam chowder and then requested that someone wheel him back into his room.

"He's doing okay. I think he'll be back at it soon enough," Susan told Natalie.

"That Wes Sheridan. He can't be beat, can he?"

"No. He sure can't," Susan lied.

After she paid a few of the Sunrise Cove bills, then shuffled over to say hello to Zach and Christine, and hurriedly delivered lunch to Scott, where he repaired yet another wardrobe closet in an upstairs room, Susan drove back to the Sheridan house. Her plan was to cook lunch for Amanda, Audrey, and Wes and to make sure everyone ate enough— enough for baby, enough for depression, enough for healing.

There was just too much to be done.

But when Susan burst through the back door, she found her daughter— still in sweatpants (albeit clean ones), hovered over a big pot of what looked like chili, her hair clean and brushed and dried, with a speaker system playing an upbeat song. At the kitchen table sat both Wes and Audrey, both dressed and fresh-faced, in the midst of laughter.

"Aunt Susie!" Audrey cried as she lifted a carrot stick into the air and wagged it around. "Will you please tell your daughter here that us pregnant ladies—"

"And those over the age of seventy," Wes interjected.

"Yes. That's right. That we deserve snacks that have a little more oomph to them, you know? Carrots aren't cutting it. We're thinking— Gramps? What are we thinking?"

"Cookies," Wes affirmed.

"And crackers, of multiple varieties," Audrey added.

"And chocolate."

"Apparently, Gramps has a sweet tooth," Audrey pointed out. "Which I have to respect."

"You guys," Amanda said brightly as she stirred the chili. "I have cookies for after chili. Remember?"

Audrey turned to Grandpa Wes and muttered, "She doesn't seem to understand that we want cookies for pre-lunch, lunch, and after lunch, does she?"

Wes grumbled. "No way."

Susan placed her bag on the couch and grinned madly at everyone. Amanda pretended not to notice Susan's eyes, even as Susan's mind burned with a million questions.

How did you manage to get out of bed today?

Did you switch all your classes online? Did Rutgers penalize you?

Are you starting to regret not going back to Newark?

Is there still a chance you can have your old life?

Have you talked to Chris?

But Susan knew these questions were unfair.

Amanda was able to cook, clean, keep the house in order, and care for the people she loved who lived in it. Wasn't that enough?

"Can I help you with anything, Amanda?" Susan asked, finally.

Amanda flipped her hair and said, "No way. Nothing. Just sit. It's almost ready."

Susan found her way to the kitchen table, where Amanda poured them each a healthy portion of chili, then added a freshly-baked loaf of bread to the center of the table, along with fresh butter with little glowing salt crystals inside.

"Wow, Amanda. Did you ask Christine to drop off this bread?" Susan asked.

"Naw. I baked it. There was a sourdough starter in the fridge, I'm assuming from Christine," Amanda said.

"There she goes. A superhero," Audrey said, teasing her.

Amanda rolled her eyes and pointed her finger to the chili. "Eat. That baby needs nutrients. I watched you wolf down a whole bag of Cheez-Its again last night. It has to stop!"

They ate and laughed together, an unlikely quartet of Sheridans. Wes continued to seem in good spirits and pointed to several of the birds that stopped at the little bird feeder outside and fluttered their bright wings.

"I can't wait to get out there and see them again," he said softly.

"Good thing they come here to say hello to you," Audrey said. "It's like they know."

Hours later, after Amanda had cleaned up the chili and Wes had gone back to his room for a nap, Susan splayed out the various items from Russell's case before her at the kitchen table. She was borderline exhausted from all the events of the day, yet knew she had to tap into this singular desire: she wanted to be a lawyer again. It had always been her dream.

As Amanda marched past, she eyed the various papers in front of Susan and stopped short. Susan could feel her daughter analyzing each page. Finally, after a horrible silence, Amanda asked, "What's all this, Mom?"

Susan gave a half-shrug. "I'm just trying to get someone out of a bind. That's all."

"I see. Your lawyer hat, huh?"

"The finest of my many hats," Susan replied sarcastically. "All the more necessary now that I don't have all that hair anymore."

Amanda dropped a kiss on her mother's head and laughed. "Don't be silly. Your hair is glorious already."

"Sheridan genes, baby girl. We all have them," Susan said.

As Susan pored over the documents, she felt herself up against one strange, horrible sensation: all evidence actually did point to Russell being at least somehow involved in the stealing of the funds. He'd been on-location for a number of the purchases, which were listed to have happened from his very computer at the Chamber of Commerce. As minutes ticked past, Susan's heart beat harder, like a drum in a punk band.

Hour after hour, she went through the pages. It wasn't until she felt a hard weight on her shoulder, waking her, that she realized she'd fallen asleep, stretched out on the papers.

"Mom? Hey, Mom." Amanda's voice was soft, sweet.

"Oh, honey. Did I fall asleep?"

"You did. And I think you should head into my room and take a nap before you drive back to Scott's," Amanda suggested.

Susan furrowed her brow and blinked up at her daughter. Without thinking, she said the worst-possible words she could have said.

"You're really going to make an excellent mom someday."

Immediately, Amanda's eyes filled with tears. She fell onto the chair across from her and bent low.

Obviously, through the baking bread and the endless cleaning and the cooking and the taking care of everyone, Amanda had tried to hover above her own emotions— her feelings of loss. Her loss of marriage, of a potential family she'd probably dreamed of, over and over again.

Obviously, as Susan knew better than most, that didn't always work out. It was like walking a tightrope.

Susan reached for Amanda's hand, but Amanda swatted it away and draped her head forward. "No, no. I'm okay."

"Amanda, I really didn't mean to say that—"

"I know you didn't."

"I mean, it's true. Whenever the time comes, you will be—"

"Mom!"

"Sorry, honey." Susan heaved a sigh. She'd walked herself into a corner. She scrunched her nose and shook her head and finally said, "I'm going to go to sleep for a while. I love you, Amanda. I know you know that, but know that I will say that every day, no matter what, for the rest of my life."

Chapter Sixteen

I t wasn't like it got any easier to wake up. Amanda dropped down on the floor beside the bed in her makeshift room, then immediately stretched herself in a Downward Dog yoga pose. Everything in her mind told her: *You are unhappy. You will never be happy again. Why do you even keep trying?* The voice continued, even as she stretched longer and felt her muscles relax.

It had now been a full week since the biggest failure and embarrassment of her life. Still, she hadn't bothered to turn on her phone and had operated only from her computer when she needed the internet: changing her classes to online, emailing her teachers, and sending messages to Brittany and Piper to let them know she was all right.

> BRITTANY: Oh my God, girl. Are you never coming back?

> PIPER: You know you shouldn't let Chris get the best of you.

> BRITTANY: One of our friends saw him, by the way. At the grocery store. Apparently, he looked AWFUL.

Nope. Amanda didn't want to read any kind of news about Chris. Not yet. She wanted to operate in this other dimension, where Chris didn't exist at all. If she awoke on Martha's Vineyard, cooked breakfast for herself and Audrey and Grandpa Wes, then dove through the rest of the tasks of the day ahead, she could almost pretend that she had the same kind of life her Grandma Anna had.

Not that Anna had really liked that life. She had stepped out of her own marriage, remember? Stan Ellis existed for a reason.

Not all marriages are right.

They take work.

But I was willing to put in the work!

Amanda let out a long gasp as she erupted from her Downward Dog position and lifted her back. A few of the tendons cracked softly. On her bed, her computer pinged, and she swept up to check the new messages.

> JAKE: Hey, sis. We just got off the ferry. Should we head to the Sunrise Cove or your place?

Jake, Kristen, and the twins had arrived. Amanda bucked up, cracked her shoulders, then wrote back.

> AMANDA: Why don't you check in? I'll get the place ready. Grandpa will be happy to see you.

> JAKE: As if we even know each other...

AMANDA: And isn't this the best time to start?

Amanda could feel Jake's annoyance, even without his answer. She dropped her phone to the mattress and then headed out toward the kitchen, where she began to bake up another loaf of bread, some cookies, and a big vat of pesto pasta. As she cooked, Audrey appeared at the bottom of the staircase with her hand on her stomach, and her lips widened into a massive yawn.

"Good morning. What's up?"

"Jake and his family are on their way," Amanda said.

"Oh, right. I forgot your overly-handsome and successful older brother was on his way," Audrey teased. She collected a scone from the little basket on the counter and dove in.

"Ha. Yes. Jake, the engineer, and Kristen, his doting teacher-wife," Amanda replied.

To her surprise, her heart felt black with both resentment and jealousy. She'd never, ever felt these things toward her brother and his wife. She had only ever loved them.

What kind of monster was she turning into?

"Good thing you started showering," Audrey remarked. It was almost like she had taken the words out of Amanda's mouth.

Amanda gave a dry laugh. "You don't have to point out everyone's flaws, you know."

Audrey shrugged. "If I do, then you're less likely to focus on mine. You know. Like, how I'm pregnant at nineteen with a guy I hardly know."

"You're the only one who ever brings that up, Aud. Not me."

"Why is Jake here again? He wasn't so keen on the Vineyard last year," Audrey said.

"I think he feels guilty that I was stood up at my own

wedding," Amanda affirmed as she kneaded the bread. "And probably, guilty about not being around so much when Mom had cancer? I don't know. He was always closer to dad, and I know he kind of resented Mom for not sticking around Newark for free babysitting."

"What! Susan Sheridan, a free babysitter? That's crazy," Audrey said in mock surprise. "Mom says she's getting back into the criminal lawyer game."

Amanda grunted. "Well, she had better drop one of her many other activities then. I keep catching her falling asleep on the table."

"Look at you. Our Sheridan Mother hen," Audrey teased. "Grandma Anna would be so proud."

"And look at you. Wearing Grandma Anna's robe like you don't own tons of maternity clothes," Amanda replied.

"I think it suits my complexion," Audrey said.

"It suits all of our complexions. We're all Anna's twin," Amanda stated. Still, her smile was electric. She loved these daily banters with Audrey.

They were the best form of medicine she could get in a time like this.

About two hours later, Jake, Kristen, and the twins entered the house, with a chorus of screeching from the twins.

"Samantha! Cody!" Audrey cried with big eyes as she greeted them.

Jake came next, ushering the twins forward. He stopped to hug Amanda and beamed, "Wow. This place smells delicious!" before he moved on to Audrey and hugged her gingerly. Kristen came next, with big gray circles beneath her eyes and, of course, a platter of brownies, which she had apparently baked on a whim.

"We always have enough food to go around," Amanda said, words that seemed to come straight from her mother.

"Where's Mom?" Jake asked.

"She's at the Sunrise Cove. You must have just missed each other. She'll be back for lunch," Amanda explained as she checked on the pasta.

A few minutes later, Amanda helped Wes roll out into the kitchen and living area, where he greeted everyone warmly and impressively and got everyone's names right. He shook Jake's hand, looked him in the eye, and said, "You know, son? You don't look at all like any Sheridan I've ever seen. I guess you're just your dad, through and through."

Jake looked a bit embarrassed at that. He glanced at Amanda, who shrugged and mouthed, "Don't worry about it."

Everyone had let bygones be bygones when it came to Richard Harris. At least, most everyone had.

* * *

After lunch, Kristen and Audrey both excused themselves upstairs while Wes took to his room with a book. Susan made her way back to the Sunrise Cove, saying, "Natalie keeps messing up the computer!" This left only Amanda and Jake— the original Harris siblings, along with the twins, who rolled around on the floor with a few toys, which they happily drooled all over.

"Wow. Look at where you live," Jake said as Amanda filled up a pot with water and began to scrub.

Amanda cast Jake a dark look. "Be careful."

Jake shook his head hurriedly and said, "No. I mean. I don't mean it in any negative way. It's obviously beautiful here. But, yeah, I mean, it's only been a week since..." He trailed off. He sensed he'd "stepped in it."

Amanda continued to scrub. God, she loved watching as the goopy pesto eased away from the now-shining pot.

"Anyway. How is it? Here?" he asked. He placed his hand at the back of his neck and gave Amanda a look that reminded

Amanda of a much younger version of Jake. In many ways, they were still kids, just trying to make it work.

Amanda shrugged. "It's cozy. I make Grandpa and Audrey lunch. I help Mom with various things. I signed up for online classes. I don't know. I guess I'm just... here. Trying not to think about it all too much."

Suddenly, Samantha yanked a toy from Cody, which caused Cody to let out a wild yelp. Jake jumped toward the scene of the crime and patiently calmed his children. Amanda looked on, impressed.

"You're getting good at that."

Jake shrugged as he splayed Cody across his chest. The toddler tucked his head across Jake's shoulder. "I guess I had to get that way." He studied Amanda for a long time before he added, "I shouldn't tell you this, but Kristen's pregnant again."

Something cold and hard formed in Amanda's stomach. How was it possible that so many lives had gone on without her? How was it possible that her mother could be engaged, and her father could have another baby, and even her brother could build his family— all while she did what?

Got dumped at the altar?

She wanted to throw the pot across the room.

My God, how her feelings changed so swiftly.

"She's not very happy about it," Jake confessed softly. "We can hardly handle these two. We didn't exactly plan for a third."

What I would do to have children.

They were on my list.

My starter house. My perfect husband. My first baby.

All gone.

Amanda wiped down her hands with a dishcloth and then walked over to Jake. She sat cross-legged across from him and Cody, alongside Samantha, and heaved a sigh. She didn't want to show Jake the darkness in her heart. She knew the more babies, the more love there would be.

Jealousy or no jealousy, this was always true.

"You've got this, Jake," Amanda said solemnly. "And I never lie."

Jake chuckled. "Has Dad told you about his?"

Amanda nodded and splayed her hands over her cheeks. "Now, if I have to tell the truth about that one— it seems kind of like a disaster."

"A new baby brother or sister," Jake said, wide-eyed as he shook his head.

"Yep. From step-mommy, Penelope."

"I can't imagine," Jake scoffed.

"But I guess we'll just have to live it. It's coming straight for us. And Dad seems way too tired to take it on."

"That's true. I thought he was going to break down when he told me," Jake confessed. "But I told him we could do it together. He kind of liked the sound of that."

"You guys will have such a weird community there in Newark. Your baby's uncle or aunt, growing up right there."

Jake furrowed his brow. "So you're really set on this, then? Martha's Vineyard?"

Amanda's lips dropped into a frown. She hadn't wanted to reveal everything to him, but here he was, giving her so much of himself.

"I don't know anything anymore, Jake. I just can't go back there right now. That's all."

Jake nodded somberly. "Okay. Let me know if you need anything. Really. I mean it, sis."

* * *

Several hours later, after Jake, Kristen, Samantha, and Cody had returned to the Sunrise Cove, Amanda perched in the kitchen and stared out at the frigid late-January Vineyard Sound. Her mind hummed with fear and anxiety. Suddenly, with the kitchen clean and everyone fed, she felt an overwhelming amount of loss and dread.

What was she if she couldn't care for others?

She knew this was only a bump in the road— a huge one at that. One she didn't feel that she would ever recover from. Somehow, though, she would find a way to keep going. Somehow.

Suddenly, her grandfather's voice erupted from beneath the crack in the door of his bedroom. Amanda was pulled out of her reverie, jumped up immediately, and opened the door to find him stretched out in bed. His arms were high over his head, and his eyes searched the ceiling, as though he was frightened of something. Amanda appeared beside him and gently took his hand to try and soothe him.

"Grandpa? Grandpa, it's me. It's Amanda."

Wes's eyes searched hers for a long moment. Slowly, his cry calmed down, easing into a croak and then into silence. He shook his head ominously against the pillow.

"I'm sorry, Amanda. I think I had a nightmare."

"It's okay, Grandpa." How could she possibly explain to him that she felt the same way, but only about her waking life?

Amanda collapsed in her grandfather's wheelchair, there beside the bed, and adjusted the blankets over him. "Do you want to get up for the afternoon?"

Wes shook his head again. "No. Not yet. I kind of want to go back to that dream, to be honest with you. Anna was there, and she'd made this perfect blackberry pie. I always loved her pies. I know she resented baking them sometimes. Especially now, I know she wasn't always so keen on the wife and mother role, you know? But when I spotted her over the top of one of those pies, so beautiful and youthful and alive, I felt something in my heart. I knew that I loved her and that it was the kind of love nobody could take away from me. And I now know that's true. Because I still feel it, even though she's been gone so long."

Amanda's eyes sparkled for a moment and she gripped her grandfather's hand a little tighter as she marveled at his impeccable memory, even in the midst of his dementia.

Slowly, Wes turned his head and nestled it so that his eyes found Amanda's once again.

"I think I want to say something to you, Amanda. But I don't want you to take offense."

Amanda nodded. Her stomach curdled strangely. "It's okay, Grandpa. You can tell me anything. I won't get offended."

Wes cleared his throat. "Marriage is a whole lot harder than you think. Maybe the fact that you didn't marry this boy at your young age was a blessing in disguise. I hope you consider it that way, in fact. He's given you a path toward a different kind of future. Maybe one day, you'll be able to thank him for it."

Amanda gave him a small smile as she patted his hand and watched him drift back to sleep. She stood and made her way to the door. Maybe, just maybe, he was right. But Amanda had a feeling that she wouldn't find a way to believe in it any time soon.

Chapter Seventeen

W hen Jake, Kristen, and the twins were on the Vineyard, Susan was able to spend maybe five hours, total over a span of two days with them. With each conversation, her heart tugged her in other directions; her anxiety was at a new height. *You have to go over Russell's case!* And her feet tugged her back to the Sunrise Cove, where she had to assist Natalie with check-ins and guest requests and any odd, random horror that occurred. Such was the life of a part-time lawyer and full-time hotelier. Such was the life of Susan Sheridan.

About a week after Jake left, Susan stood at the Sunrise Cove desk, with her work stretched out in front of her. Somewhere deep inside her, she prayed that nobody would tumble down that staircase and demand anything from her; she felt hyper-focused on the task at-hand and just couldn't possibly deal with a "we need more toilet paper" or a "can you please come change our lightbulb?" situation.

Over the previous week, Susan had burrowed herself into Russell's case. She had analyzed every single receipt, made copies of the guest book at the Chamber of Commerce, and interviewed Russell's colleagues. To her surprise, the colleagues were generally split about what they thought had happened. A few of them seemed kind of jealous of Russell's position and were more than willing to throw him under the bus.

"If you ask me, Russell has always had his eyes set on higher plans for himself," one of them told her. "It doesn't shock me at all that he stole Chamber of Commerce funds and used them for whatever he pleased. In his mind, he deserves it."

Others, on the other hand, saw the Russell that Susan really felt was the real man who'd dedicated so many years of service to the community— although who could really be sure?

"I was with Russell for a lot of the past six months," one little old lady said, "and I never saw him do anything like this. He only handled funds for the town of Oak Bluffs and the Vineyard at large. I would have put a stop to it if I'd caught him doing anything else."

Susan dropped her forehead to the desk below and racked her mind. She'd pored over these documents night after night yet still couldn't come up with any kind of shadow of a doubt that Russell hadn't been the one to make these purchases. Saying, "He's just such a good guy!" had never really worked in court. She'd never even tried it because, well... she was a damn good lawyer.

At least, she had been a good lawyer back in Newark.

"Hey there." The voice was familiar and warm, and it drew Susan's head back up from the counter. She blinked at Scott, who carried over two chocolate chip cookies and two glasses of milk. He placed them in front of her and said, "I don't think I've had a chance to talk to you since last night."

Susan blinked away her sleepiness. "Scott, these cookies look delicious. Thank you."

"Don't thank me. Your sister baked them and insisted I bring them over to you. What were her words? Something like,

'She's burning the candle at both ends.'" Scott's eyes twinkled knowingly. "Of course, we both agreed that you wouldn't do this if you didn't really care about it."

Susan buzzed her lips as she lifted a cookie. "Wow. She even put sea salt on them. She's so good at what she does."

"You're avoiding the conversation, aren't you?"

Susan shrugged playfully and dug her teeth into the edge of the outer crust, which gave way to the inner goo of the cookie. "Did you stop by Dad's place this afternoon?"

Scott allowed her to side-step the conversation, at least for now. "Yep. Everything seems normal on their end. Amanda's concocted yet another healthy recipe for your dad and Audrey, and Audrey and Wes are doing very slow laps, back and forth, in the living room. They think he'll have his strength back relatively soon."

"Good kids," Susan said somberly. "I don't know what I would do without them right now."

"I know what you would do. You would collapse," Scott affirmed.

Susan rolled her eyes and shoved the plate of cookies toward him. "Come on. Eat your cookie."

Scott shook his head. "That second one is for you, too. I know you'll be up late tonight, so save it for later."

"Hey." Susan's heart felt full with the way Scott always thought about her. She reached out, gripped Scott's hand, and held it tenderly. His eyes met hers, and again, she felt that jump in her gut. It was proof that she loved him so completely, so wonderfully, with every fiber of her being. "I promise it won't be like this forever. I just want to see if I can still do this."

Scott nodded somberly. "I know."

"I love you so much. And I can't wait to marry you."

Scott's mouth cracked into a handsome grin. "I know."

"And we'll even set a date soon. I promise."

"Susan. We have all the time in the world," Scott told her. "I just want you to be happy."

* * *

Later that night, as Amanda scrubbed up the pots, pans, and dinner plates and Wes retired for the evening, Susan again set up shop at the kitchen table with all her documents. Audrey splayed out across the living room floor and moaned, "I really miss that stupid cat. I wish Christine hadn't taken him to Zach's." She then propped her head upon her hand and blinked at Susan. "Do you think I should be doing something else to prepare for this baby? Like, should I be knitting a tiny hat, or writing some kind of letter, or..."

Amanda chuckled from the kitchen as she eased a towel over a large pot. "I would pay good money to watch you knit a hat."

Audrey stuck out her tongue playfully at her cousin. "I'll have you know I can be pretty crafty when the mood strikes me."

Susan chuckled inwardly but turned her eyes back to the pages before her. The last time she had spoken with Russell, his face had seemed so shadowed; his cheeks had been drawn in. She owed it to his mental health and the mental health of Claire to keep going.

But she felt stumped and so at a loss. She couldn't find the evidence she needed to prove his innocence.

Over the next hour, she continued to make notes for herself, to try to construct something out of the material she had gathered. Throughout, Amanda and Audrey gossiped and flipped through magazines on the floor. Susan had noticed that all the wedding magazines had been recycled; now, there were only fashion magazines, gossip magazines, entertainment magazines, the kinds of things young women loved.

For whatever reason, this warmed her heart. Maybe it was the first step toward Amanda's healing.

Susan knew it would be a long, long road.

After Audrey went up to bed, Amanda sat across from Susan and poured them both a glass of wine. She blinked at the print-outs, the photographs of the guest book, and the various transcripts from interviews Susan had conducted. "Any luck?" she asked.

Susan shook her head so that her curls wafted over her ears. "I just don't know how to put a reasonable doubt into these people's heads. Normally, it comes so easily for me. I guess I've just lost my touch? I don't know."

Amanda's voice was soft. "Do you mind if I take a look?"

With her chair pulled up alongside Susan's, Amanda walked herself through what Susan had so far of the case. Her eyes shimmered with excitement as she asked questions, made connections that Susan had already made, and added up various receipts. For well over an hour, Susan gave Amanda the bones of the deal— more or less wringing out her own mind of details.

But suddenly, Amanda flung her hand forward and gripped one of the receipts, along with one of the guest book print-outs.

"Mom! Look at this."

Susan furrowed her brow as Amanda splayed both items before her. "This is the date that the speed boat was purchased. See? And it says it was purchased from a computer at the Chamber of Commerce. Russell's computer, in fact. It has the IP stamp."

"Yes..."

"But look! Look at the guest book."

Susan did. And when she did, her eyes nearly fell out of her head.

"Russell wasn't there that day," Susan breathed.

"Nope." Excitement flashed across Amanda's face, making

her look more alive than she had in weeks. Hurriedly, she investigated some of the other items. Each and every one lined up with a date when Russell wasn't actually in the office; otherwise, the item had been purchased in the hours after he'd signed out.

Susan gaped at her daughter. "I can't believe this."

Amanda rubbed her palms together excitedly. "There it is! I think that's proof!"

"Amanda, it's everything I've been searching for the past few weeks."

"I mean, and look at this—" Amanda continued, furrowing her brow as she dove through another sign-in list. "It looks like Mike, of all people, was around for a lot of these."

"Mike? Like, Kelli's Mike?"

"Yes. That horrible man," Amanda said. "I can't believe he did this to his own brother-in-law. Do you think it's possible he was scheming his way off the island the whole time?"

"What perfect timing after verbally assaulting Kelli."

Amanda shrugged. "I don't know if we could fully prove it was him, though."

"But we have a reasonable doubt it wasn't Russell," Susan said.

Amanda and Susan exchanged enormous smiles. Susan flung herself forward, wrapped her daughter in a big hug, and breathed the first sigh of relief she'd had in ages.

"I don't know why I didn't ask you for help sooner," Susan said as the hug broke. "I just wanted to do it all on my own."

"I know that instinct. I have the same one," Amanda replied, flashing a wink at her mother.

"Hence all the cleaning and cooking and taking care of everyone?"

"It's what you would have done if you had the time," Amanda said with a shrug.

"Is there anything you can't do?" Susan asked with a laugh.

Amanda's eyes darkened at this. Susan could almost feel the words rolling around in her mind. *Marry the love of my life. Start a family— all the things I always wanted to do.*

But instead of allowing her daughter to dwell, Susan said suddenly, "Why don't you continue to help me with the case? I would have gone crazy without you tonight. No reason why you can't be in the room with me when we defend Russell."

Amanda's eyes held hers for a long time. "I'd really like that, Mom."

Chapter Eighteen

The court proceedings for Oak Bluffs versus Russell Whalen lasted no more than twenty minutes. Within that time, Amanda and her mother were able to prove that not only was Russell not to blame for the enormous funds that had been spent at the expense of the taxpayers, but they also hinted that someone had set up Russell Whalen. Someone related to the Montgomery family. They reported that they would turn over their findings to the prosecution for them to dig deeper into this mess. They were grateful that the proceedings were fluid. Amanda spoke, then Susan, until finally, the judge ruled that he couldn't see enough evidence to convict Russell of what he'd been accused of.

"As you all know, I must be presented with enough evidence in order to rule a conviction. Prior to these proceedings, it seemed clear that Russell Whalen was the only one whose hands could have committed these crimes, as it seemed clear he was the only one able to access most of these funds," Judge Harriett said. "However, thanks to Ms. Sheridan and Miss Harris, it's become clear to me that this has moved entirely in the incorrect direction. I hereby declare Russell Whalen not guilty. Russell, you have been an upstanding member of this community for a number of years. I hope you won't see this brief time as a bruise on all you've accomplished. We appreciate you, and we see your worth. Thank you."

Outside, Susan flung her arms around Amanda and breathed, "That was incredible, Mandy!" into her ear.

Amanda, for one, wanted to jump up and down with excitement. She hadn't felt that good in what felt like months. She leaned back from her mother's embrace and grinned madly, then turned back to find Russell, Claire, Uncle Trevor, Aunt Kerry, Everett, Charlotte, Kelli, Steven, and Andy, who'd all come to watch the proceedings. They all beamed at Susan and Amanda. Aunt Kerry looked on the verge of tears.

Russell stepped toward Amanda and Susan and cleared his throat. He didn't seem to be the kind of man who broke down easily, but when he opened his mouth, his voice cracked strangely, as though he really might this time.

"Seriously, Susan, Amanda, I don't know how I can possibly thank you."

Aunt Kerry smacked her hands together and called out, "I know how I can start!"

Kelli chuckled softly and linked her arm with Andy's. "She's going to say she made enough clam chowder for all of us."

"Don't give it all away, Kelli," Aunt Kerry stuttered. Her glove found her cheek and wiped another tear away. "I wanted it to be a surprise."

"Christine's got everything set up back at your place," Charlotte announced brightly. "We thought it would be a good time for a proper Sheridan and Montgomery family dinner—regardless of what the results would have been."

"And the results were nothing but spectacular," Uncle

Trevor affirmed. "Although, this news about Mike being the potential criminal and setting up a family member..."

Kelli grumbled. "Let's not talk about that quite yet. I don't know if I have it in me to consider that he actually went that far."

They fell into line together and walked back to their various parked cars. Aunt Kerry landed herself close to Susan and Amanda. Through tears, she whispered, "When you first called to say you suspected Mike, I told Kelli immediately, and she asked her daughter to come live with us. I had wanted her to do that from the get-go, but of course, Kelli didn't want to disrupt her daughter's last year of school."

"I wondered if she would do that," Susan said. "I don't blame her."

"Do you think they'll investigate him?" Aunt Kerry asked.

"Absolutely. Especially after the evidence we brought in today, they'll have to," Susan told her. "Although we never know what goes on in the minds of prosecutors."

Aunt Kerry clucked her tongue. "Listen to you. You sound like a real lawyer, Susan Sheridan."

Amanda's mother beamed and linked her arm with Amanda's.

Amanda answered for her. "She is a real lawyer, Aunt Kerry. I grew up thinking she was the smartest woman in the world. Now, I just know for a fact she is."

The cars and trucks piled themselves outside the Sheridan house. Amanda hopped out of her mother's car and hustled in to find Audrey, nibbling on a cookie and watching the *Last Holiday* with tears running down her cheeks. Beside her was Grandpa Wes, who seemed similarly captivated.

"What happened!" Audrey asked with the cookie poised in front of her. "Did you get his name cleared?"

Here, without the others seeing, Amanda did a little jig of joy. Audrey slowly drew herself to a standing position and then threw her arms around her cousin. "That's the badass Amanda I know and love," she whispered. "Good job. I know Aunt Susan couldn't have done it without you."

Wes seemed a bit confused about the whole affair, but he, too, stood up and gave Amanda a well-meaning hug. As he scratched the back of his head and prepared to ask a question, the others stomped into the house, removed their boots, and greeted Audrey and Grandpa Wes with uplifted "Hello!"s and "We did it!"s.

"Well, actually, your beautiful, talented, successful, and intelligent daughter and granddaughter did it," Aunt Kerry announced as she headed into the living room and hugged her brother close. "I don't know what we did to deserve such a wonderful family."

The clam chowder was already cooked. Christine appeared from upstairs to hug everyone and get the last of the rolls out of the oven. Scott stomped in a few minutes later, along with Zach, Lola, and Tommy. Soon after, Steven announced that his wife, Laura, was on her way, and Kelli said her daughter planned to stop by soon.

"We're going to stuff this place to the gills all over again," Aunt Kerry said as she headed toward the back closet. There, she found another table, nestled in there from Christmastime. Amanda leaped forward to help her undo it and prop it up in the living room.

"Thanks, Amanda," Aunt Kerry said. Her eyes studied Amanda's for a long time.

It struck Amanda that maybe, she hadn't had much one-on-one time with her Great-Aunt Kerry. She struggled under the weight of her gaze. *What does this older woman think of me, now that I've been left at the altar alone? Should I be embarrassed? Does she think I've failed?*

But instead, she dipped her head low and said, "You're a

businesswoman beyond anything, aren't you? A different kind of woman from a different generation. I have to respect that. And in some ways, it makes me jealous. I love my family, and I love my husband, but when I got into the real estate business, I had a knack for it that surprised me. I closed a number of deals Uncle Trevor might have lost out on. That's just between you and me." She grinned wildly, and before turning, she winked at Amanda.

Amanda laughed at that. Warmth flowed through her as she fell into Aunt Kerry's compliment like it was a cloud.

Nobody cared that she wasn't going to marry Chris.

Nobody cared for anything but her happiness.

That was why she loved her family so much.

Together, the Sheridan and Montgomery families (along with the many people who loved them) sat and ate and drank wine and laughed together. Occasionally, Kelli got up to "act out" Susan and Amanda's conversation with the judge so that the others could see them in their true "lawyer" fashion. Midway through her performance, Andy got up to play the part of the judge, which made everyone burst into laughter, especially because he soon morphed the character into a much more cartoonish judge character. Just as he flung a little towel over his head to make an old-fashioned "judge wig," like you see on TV, Beth and her son, Will, walked in to find him all dressed up with a silly grin on his face.

Beth burst into laughter the second she spotted him, while Will, who had autism, just blinked at him strangely.

"Andy. What do you have on your head?" he asked, as though it was the simplest question in the world.

Everyone at the table burst into laughter yet again. Andy dropped down, still with that towel in his hand, and said, "Do you think it makes me look dignified? Important?"

At this, Will gave Andy one of his rare smiles and then joined everyone else in giggling. Andy stepped past Will and kissed Beth on the cheek as she removed the towel from his head.

"How was the hospital?" he asked.

"Just fine," she said. "Hello, everyone!"

"Beth, I hope you're hungry," Aunt Kerry said.

"Always," Beth replied with a smile. "Especially when it comes to your clam chowder."

Amanda began to remove people's bowls to pile them in the sink for later. Audrey joined her at the counter and beamed out across the families as the chatter and boisterous laughter streamed past them.

"Isn't it weird?" Audrey asked suddenly. She placed her hands on her back and leaned into them to puff out her stomach even more.

"What exactly?" Amanda returned.

"It's just that everything has changed so quickly from last year. I mean, a year ago, I lived in a dorm and I drank beer on Friday nights and I kissed cute fraternity boys. And now, I spend my Friday nights watching movies with Grandpa Wes— who, I might add, probably didn't even know I existed until last June."

Amanda chuckled at the truth in her words, even as her heart burned with sadness for the life she had so desperately wanted back in Newark. She could practically see herself in another dimension: preparing dinner for Chris as she finalized another law school project.

"You know, I hope you don't think that was just some kind of small-town thing." Susan appeared in the kitchen and peered at Amanda, her voice low.

Amanda placed the rest of the bowls in the sink and turned fully to meet her mother's eyes. Audrey stepped back toward the fridge and then escaped, sensing an "important conversation" brewing.

"What do you mean?" Amanda asked.

Susan tilted her wine glass to make the liquid flow in circles. She stepped closer to Amanda and kept her voice low to ensure the others at the tables couldn't hear her.

"That case wasn't so easy. It wasn't so simple. It wasn't just 'Oak Bluffs small town silliness.' It had depth to it. And you conquered it easily."

Amanda's cheeks burned at the compliment. "Thank you for saying that."

Susan shrugged. "I mean it." She sipped her wine and then returned the empty glass to the counter. "You should know that I wasn't exactly pleased with your decision to go online after what happened."

Amanda's nostrils flared. Here it was: the truth.

"But I knew, somewhere in all this, you'd done what was right for you."

"It hasn't been easy," Amanda told her. "But I think it was what I needed. Is what I need, I mean."

"What if I started my own firm?" Susan said suddenly.

"Your own firm?"

"Yes. I know how it goes because your father and I had our own firm back in Newark. This would be just me, Susan Sheridan, with a potential intern who eventually might agree to be my partner. Somewhere down the line— after she passes the bar."

Amanda's eyes grew enormous when she finally understood her mother's words. She gaped at her mother, her superhero, the woman she had always aspired to be, and marveled at the idea of this brand-new life:

A partner in a law firm—a partner to her mother, Susan Sheridan.

A life on the island, surrounded by loved ones.

Maybe it was an answer to something.

"It sounds so wonderful, Mom, but I'll have to think about it," she told her mother, even as her heart fluttered in her chest.

"Take all the time you need," Susan assured her. "I know it's a big decision."

Later that evening, as the family continued to gather around the table, chat, and drink wine, Amanda marched into the bedroom she had taken over the past few weeks. Slowly, with a heavy hand, she grabbed the phone that had been black as night since the Sunday she was stood up at the altar, and she plugged it into the charger.

In minutes, it pinged with countless messages.

"Hey, girl! I hope you're okay. I heard what happened and I—"

"MANDY! I heard you dropped our class together. I can't—"

"Amanda, I just talked to Chris about the rent. Can you send it—"

"Miss Harris, this is about your request to change your last name—"

After the wave finished, Amanda smiled to herself. Chris hadn't sent her a single message. This both surprised and didn't surprise her. After all, he was probably just as numb and shocked and feeling strange about it all as she was. Probably more, since he had been the one to cause it. She could only imagine the flack his mother had given him. In fact, the idea of it made Amanda laugh aloud.

Finally, she pressed her thumbs to the screen and wrote:

> AMANDA: Hey, Chris. Longtime, no talk.

> AMANDA: And by that, I mean, I think we need to talk.

Chapter Nineteen

Scott and Susan hovered outside the truck window. Amanda was reminded of how nervous Susan and Richard had looked four and a half years before, when she'd gone off for undergraduate school, making them empty nesters. She had seen the fear reflected in their eyes— the fact that their baby was leaving for her own adventure to find herself.

This was different, in a way, but not by much.

Amanda rolled down the window to speak with Scott and Susan one final time before she wheeled off.

"The seat all adjusted?" Scott asked, anxious. "It can sometimes stick."

"I think I got it," Amanda told him.

"And the radio? You can change that to whatever you want. I don't have any kind of way to hook up your phone or..."

"That's okay," Amanda replied. "I love the radio."

"And you know the way?" Susan asked suddenly, then whipped her hand over her mouth and shook her head. "I'm sorry," she murmured as Amanda chuckled. "I don't know why

I'm nervous. I guess it's because I've seen you every day the past few weeks, and now you're headed off. I'm going to miss you."

"Just one night, Mom," Amanda said as she tried out a smile. "It'll fly by."

"Good luck over there," Susan told her. "Call me if you need anything. And remember, I can still jump in this truck right now and come over to help."

"I'll tell you what I've already told you and Aunt Lola and Audrey and Aunt Christine and even Charlotte and Claire," Amanda said with a laugh. "I have to do this by myself. But I appreciate the offer. I really do."

Amanda had never taken a car across the ferry. Of course, as she eased it up over the ramp, the guy working waved and hollered, "Hey, Scott!" then immediately changed his face, rapped on the window, and asked her to roll it down. "You are decidedly not Scott Frampton," he said with a smile.

"My mom is Susan Sheridan," Amanda explained. "Scott lent me the truck for the night. I have to move my stuff back from Newark."

"Oh!" Although Amanda had never seen this man before, a story played out across his face— one that told her he knew exactly who she was. *The jilted bride. Well, whatever. It didn't matter.* "Well, carry on, then. Scott has a year-round pass to take the truck back and forth, so lucky you."

The drive back to Newark was a strange one. Amanda gripped the steering wheel so hard that her knuckles began to ache, and she switched back and forth on so many radio stations that she nearly did her head in with the variety of genres. Rock to country to soft rock to old-school rock— she couldn't make up her mind. Rock had never been particularly "her thing," but there was something about the loud music that allowed her to forget what she was about to do and just get lost in the moment.

Here I go. I'm about to meet my ex-fiancé for the first time since he left me at the altar.

It was both a nightmare and a rom-com. Audrey had said multiple times that although she probably couldn't have lifted much of Amanda's stuff, she really wanted to be there to see what was said. "I hope you throw a brick at his head," she'd added. "He deserves it."

Amanda parked the truck outside of the familiar Newark apartment just as the sun disappeared beneath the horizon. When she stopped the engine, she felt a profound sense of loss. After all, hadn't she parked in this very spot, arrived "home" to this apartment so many times, all without a second thought? This was the final time. It was difficult to know how to feel.

When Amanda reached the apartment door, she didn't have time to knock or ring the bell before Chris opened it. It shocked Amanda to see him, mostly because it didn't shock her at all. Here he was: not a monster, but the same-old, same-old Chris, who wore a V-neck black t-shirt she had bought for him at Target and a pair of jeans. As he pulled the door open further, she noticed that his feet were bare, and for whatever reason, this nearly made her cry. There was something so intimate about someone's bare feet.

Maybe this would be the last time she would ever see them.

"Hey," she heard herself say as she stepped forward and hugged him. He hugged her back, but it felt a bit stunted, lacking the warmth it normally held. They hadn't been intimate with one another during the week of their wedding. At the time, Amanda had thought this was because they'd wanted to make their wedding night special.

"Hey," Chris returned as their hug broke. He stepped back to guide her into the place she knew better than her own hand. "How was the drive?"

Amanda could hardly answer. Her throat felt tight and strange. Behind Chris, she saw a number of boxes, already packaged up and complete with labels, like AMANDA'S BOOKS, AMANDA'S CLOTHES, and AMANDA'S KITCHEN STUFF.

"Wow, Chris. You already have my boxes packed," she said, feeling a little stunned by the notion.

Chris gave a half-shrug. "I don't know. I didn't want you to have to do all of it after you drove so far. It's um. Well. It was the least I could do."

There was silence for a moment. Amanda walked toward the first pile of boxes and, for the first time, felt the enormous undertaking of moving all this away from the place she'd wanted to spend her life. Some of it would go to her dad's place, stocked away in her old bedroom, while the rest, she would bring with her to Martha's Vineyard. How strange, stupid, and bizarre.

"Can I, um. Get you a glass of wine?" Chris asked.

Amanda nodded without thinking. "Yes. I would like that."

When Amanda and Chris had first moved into the apartment, their furniture had been three days late, lodged away in some warehouse somewhere. For those days, they had laughed and drank on the floor of the living room, both amazed that they'd built this life for themselves.

For this reason, Amanda dropped down to the ground, crossed her legs, and leaned back against the couch. Chris laughed. It was a sound Amanda hadn't heard in quite some time (maybe not for a year or more, since he'd taken on so much more at work). He joined her with two glasses of wine and then placed the bottle beside them. When his eyes met hers, Amanda's heart dropped into her stomach.

How the heck could they even begin to discuss what had happened?

"Oh. This Cabernet. I always liked it," Amanda commented instead, inspecting the bottle.

"I know. I got it from that wine shop you like."

"Right, the lady with that little poodle."

"The poodle recently died, unfortunately."

"Oh." Amanda studied her glass of wine. Again, she wanted to burst into tears.

"I heard you took some time off of school?" Chris said, palming the back of his neck.

"Not really. I'm just doing online classes for now and helping my mom set up her law office," Amanda said. "It's kind of been a whirlwind, but we already have a few clients, and well. Yeah. We're supposed to look at offices next week."

"Wow." Chris shook his head tentatively.

"What?"

"It's just. Well. You've already made a life for yourself, it seems like."

Mostly cleaning, cooking, and caring for Grandpa Wes. Mostly crying about you. Mostly wondering why you left me.

"It's just the classic Amanda Harris way, I guess. I don't know why I'm surprised," Chris said.

Amanda wanted to laugh, but she knew the laugh would sound unkind, and she didn't want to be angry. Not now.

"How is work?" Amanda asked, finally. She shifted against the couch and brought her elbow up over the side. Her eyes flitted across the muscles of his t-shirt with the memory of what she'd once known so well.

"It's um. Well. Actually." Chris shook his head, seemingly exasperated. "I actually just put in my two weeks' notice."

Amanda's jaw dropped. "Chris! What?" Her first reaction revolved around ideas like *That promotion was everything you wanted! It was going to set us up for the perfect life! How could you mess this up?*

Chris sighed. "I don't know. I can't explain much of it— any of this, Amanda." He bit his lower lip softly and then proceeded. "I don't think I've been straight-forward about what I've wanted for a really long time, and I really regret that. I owe you the biggest apology. I don't think I can ever, ever apologize enough for what I did to you, Amanda. I. Am. So. Sorry."

Amanda knew, in the bottom of her heart, that he meant it.

She also wasn't fully sure she could forgive him. Maybe never.

"I think you're one of the most amazing people I've ever met, Amanda," Chris continued. His eyes filled with tears. "Every night, I told myself how lucky I was that you wanted to build this life with me. You wanted to be my wife and have my children. You wanted to put up with me— me and all my stupidities and the fact that I really insisted we get this couch, which you were right, is totally the wrong color for the room."

Oh, great. Now, Amanda started to cry. Tears rolled down her cheeks. She remembered that argument and weirdly wanted to return to it, if only to return to the feeling of being in love, of knowing what that truly felt like, and of being in a team with Chris.

"But there is something about my life that doesn't add up for me right now," Chris said. He bowed his head low and shook it. "The wedding, the promotion, and all those lists you drew up?"

The stupid lists.

"It was so much pressure. I couldn't stop thinking of all the things I still wanted to do. Things like traveling to Australia or studying a foreign language. Things like, I don't know— moving to California for a while. I don't know."

Amanda marveled at his words. She hadn't heard Chris say anything about any of it. Not Australia. Not California. Nothing.

"Why didn't you say something?" she whispered.

Chris's eyes told her everything she needed to know.

She just didn't fit in those plans.

And, if she was fully honest with herself, she didn't want to fit into those plans. She had to build a life of her own.

144

After a glass of wine, she and Chris loaded the boxes into Scott's truck. They did it mostly in silence but made occasional jokes, which seemed even funnier than they should have since the emotion of it all was so intense. When they'd finally finished, Amanda watched Chris latch ropes over the top of the boxes to ensure they stayed down tight.

"You'll be safe out on the road in this big truck?" he asked. His voice was the same one he'd used when they'd been a couple, the same voice she'd imagined teaching their sons and daughters how to ride a bike.

"Yes. I'm only going to my dad's place," Amanda told him.

"That's what I thought," Chris said. "But still."

They hugged a final time. It was somber, sincere, and then it was over.

"You're going to do great things, Amanda Harris," Chris told her softly as the hug broke.

Amanda slipped into the truck and waited until Chris returned to the apartment and pressed the door closed. She expected herself to cry. She even closed her eyes and waited for it. Although there was immense pressure on her chest, the tears didn't come. She wondered what that meant. Maybe it didn't have to mean anything.

Before she drove away, Amanda lifted her phone, found Chris's contact, and hovered over it for a moment.

When he'd given her his number, she'd felt it: an entire eternity stretched out before them. She'd been so young, yet so sure of herself and of him.

Now, she wasn't sure of anything.

And with the flick of her finger, she deleted his number.

He was a part of her past, now.

Chapter Twenty

Lola blinked up at Susan from the corner of the little cabin. Paint dripped down her cheeks, coated her eyelashes, and stained her t-shirt. She shook her arms out on either side of her and opened her mouth to scream. "Oh. My. Gosh!"

Susan, who'd been busy painting the far wall with Christine, dropped her paintbrush and burst into laughter. "Lorraine! What did you do to yourself?"

"I dropped the stupid paintbrush!" Lola cried. She wrung out her hands and then reached for a nearby towel. "I don't even know what to do. It's all in my hair, and ugh. I probably look disgusting."

Christine gasped, clutched her stomach, and continued to shake with laughter.

"Christine! Have a little sympathy, okay?" Lola demanded as she pulled the towel back and glared.

"I'm sorry—" Christine cried. "You just look so—"

Lola grunted and whipped back toward the bathroom.

146

Susan and Christine exchanged glances, placed their hands over their mouths, and struggled to get through the last of the laughter in quiet.

Under her breath, Christine said, "I'm glad she at least decided to give us a show. I'm getting so bored of this wall."

"We're almost done," Susan declared. "At least, I am. I have to go check on these offices downtown."

Christine's smile was enormous. "I can't believe you arranged those on the very day we promised Little Lola we would help her paint."

"It wasn't on purpose, Christine!"

"Sure. As though Susan Sheridan would ever get the dates mixed up."

Susan placed her brush back on a plastic container, placed her hands on her hips, and analyzed the work they'd done so far. It was a crisp and gloriously blue day in mid-February, one of the days that put that jump in your heart and told you, very soon, spring would arrive and, with it, a whole host of new things.

"She's really whipped this place into shape, hasn't she?" Susan said.

"Did she show you the art she bought to hang on the walls after it's dried?" Christine asked. "I know a few of the photographers she chose. Insanely cool."

"Oh, you mean, from your artistic and fancy life back in New York?" Susan teased.

Christine rolled her eyes, then grumbled, "Well, yes."

Susan laughed. "Imagine what you could be doing instead of painting Lola's cabin? Caviar with socialites. Yacht rides with celebrities."

Christine turned back toward the wall and continued to paint. "I'm not listening!"

Lola reappeared from the bathroom. She'd gotten most of

the paint off her face but still had streaks of it in her hair. She moaned and reached for a bag of chips, which they'd splayed on the couch earlier. "Are you leaving us in a lurch, Susie?"

"I told you guys! Amanda and I want to check out some offices downtown. It would be good for us to set aside actual space for our new clients so that we don't spend so much time at the kitchen table. Audrey needs that space for her snacks, apparently."

"And Amanda would love to have somewhere else to go, I'm sure," Lola chimed in. "I talked to her a bit about what happened with Chris in Newark. It sounds kind of civil— almost beyond their years, which is quite impressive but still so sad."

"I just want to put as much distance between Chris and us as possible," Susan said firmly. She felt the stubbornness in her own voice. "No matter what his reasons are, I want him to be more of an idea than a person right now."

As Susan slid her winter coat over her shoulders, Lola analyzed the hard work they'd done that morning. "I can't believe it, but I really think when Tommy gets back from sailing, he's going to love it. The man is finally settling down. And he even complimented a few of the photographs I bought!"

"Think he'll ever pop the question?" Christine teased, grinning madly at her.

At this, Lola's cheeks burned bright red. She shifted her weight and then turned her eyes to the ground. "I don't know. I mean. I always thought maybe I didn't want that. But now..."

"But now maybe Lorraine Sheridan has had a change of heart?" Christine said.

"Haven't we all?" Lola whispered.

* * *

A shower, a sandwich, and a quick drive to downtown Oak Bluffs later, Susan found herself touring three empty rooms that had the potential to become the law offices of Sheridan and Harris (several years down the line, of course, after Amanda passed the bar). With every step she took and every question she asked the realtor, she felt this wild future stretch out before her and Amanda. Was it really possible that they could spend every day, side-by-side, discussing that which they really loved the most: the law?

"Don't get too excited, but I do have one other listing available as of this morning," the realtor told her as they walked out into the chilly February mid-day. "I thought of you first."

By the time they reached the second office space, Amanda had joined them. She wore a beautiful black pea coat, and her hair caught the bright sun beautifully. She greeted the realtor with an air of professionalism and then began to ask a range of questions about the office space, even some that Susan had forgotten to ask. Susan made a mental note to thank Amanda later for that; what would she do without her teammate?

In some respects, this reminded Susan of the first few years she'd worked alongside Richard. They'd complemented one another beautifully. Perhaps Amanda had the good attributes that her father had.

Mid-way through their tour, the realtor had to take a quick call out in the lobby. Susan and Amanda hovered in the empty space, which glowed with light from the floor-to-ceiling windows. Amanda crossed and uncrossed her arms as Susan flung hers out on either side.

"What do you think?" Susan breathed, her voice catching. "Could you see us working here?"

Amanda's eyes were glassy, as though she was on the verge of tears. "Weirdly, I really could, Mom."

"Weirdly?" Susan laughed aloud at that, then drew her arms around her daughter and held her tight against her.

When Amanda had returned from Newark a few days before, she'd taken to her bed for several hours. After that, Amanda had reappeared in the living room, her brow furrowed and her eyes stern. *I never want to leave this island,* she'd said. *I feel like it was a gift that I was even able to return here. And Chris is right. Our paths are just different now. I sensed it a long time ago. And really, I should thank him for being brave enough to do something about it.*

Susan had sensed a little bit of a lie within her daughter's words. Obviously, Amanda wouldn't get over such heartbreak so quickly. That said, Susan could feel that she was grateful not to be stuck in a marriage that wasn't true at heart. Susan knew better than most that sometimes, the words you told yourself became a path toward some kind of healing.

When the realtor returned, Susan broke the hug with her daughter, cracked her mouth into a huge grin and said, "I think this is the one."

"Really!" The realtor looked mesmerized, as though she'd never had to put less work into making a deal.

"This one is definitely the one," Susan beamed.

"Here's where we're going to hang art on the walls," Amanda added, pointing.

"And where our desks will go!" Susan continued.

"And where we'll pour wine at the end of a very long day to celebrate our victories," Amanda said, gesturing toward an empty space near the wall. "I can envision it now."

The realtor chuckled, spread out her palms, and said, "Well, okay then. Shall I draw up the paperwork?"

Susan and Amanda clasped hands and nodded in unison. "I think it's time," Susan declared.

Back at home, they found Wes with a big bag of peanut M&Ms, and Audrey stretched out on the floor near his feet with her head propped up on a pillow. Susan feigned a stern voice to her father. "Dad, what have I told you about sugar?"

At this, Audrey clucked her tongue and said, "Aunt Susie, he's helping me. I've already caught four in my mouth."

"Helping you? Are you in training or something?" Amanda asked as she stepped over her cousin.

"Yes. I'm in training to keep my mind off of the fact that I'm bigger than a whale," Audrey attested.

"She's gotten pretty good at it," Wes said. "It reminds me of my old basketball days. Your mother used to come out and watch me. All the other boys had cheerleader girlfriends, and I had my Anna." He lowered his voice conspiratorially and said, "Anna was always a little too artistic for anything like that." He then pitched the peanut M&M in a perfect parabola. It landed squarely on Audrey's tongue, and then they both burst into cheers.

"I didn't realize we walked into such a game," Susan said with a laugh.

After Audrey chewed and swallowed, she lifted her hands as a request for help back to her feet. Amanda eased her up slowly and carefully.

"You guys look happy," Audrey said. "Did you find an office space?"

"We did!" Susan cried.

Audrey clapped her hands, adjusted her shirt, and then said, "I have thought about it a lot. And I want to help you with marketing. If you're going to have these offices, then there's no reason you can't have a few social media and Google ads running, just to get your name out there."

Susan arched her eyebrow. Not for a moment had she considered that Audrey might have something professional to add to her law offices. Amanda and Susan exchanged glances; Amanda shrugged and then said, "Okay! Sure. Let's do it. After dinner?"

"After dinner," Audrey affirmed. She lifted her hand for Grandpa Wes to high-five.

"I told you they needed you," Grandpa Wes insisted. "You just doubted yourself."

Audrey pressed her finger to her lips and then hissed, "Don't give the game away, Grandpa. I have to play it cool."

"If there's anything we don't do in the Sheridan family," Susan said with a hearty laugh, "It's playing it cool."

Chapter Twenty-One

"Babe, you should have been there. Piper set it all up—wines from all over France and Italy and cheeses from Switzerland. All these really hot guys who work in the film industry were just chilling and flirting with whomever. The entire time, I couldn't help but think— why isn't Amanda here? She should be here!"

This was Brittany. She'd called Amanda that morning around ten to recount some events of the previous weekend. All Amanda, who was poring over various documents for her mother's legal firm, could do, was say, "Uh-huh. Wow. Cool," over and over again, until Brittany finally exploded and said, "Amanda, come on! When is this going to stop? When are you coming back to Newark?"

Amanda heaved a sigh and dropped her head back. "I told you. I'm going to help my mom set up her legal practice. I might come back for more in-person classes in the fall, but I'm hoping to cram them all in the middle of the week so that I can spend most of my time here. I live here now, Brittany."

Brittany was disgruntled. "I just don't understand why

Chris has to be the reason I lose you for good. It doesn't seem fair. I had all these plans for us. When I finally got myself a boyfriend and we all settled down together..."

"I know. I had dreams like that, too. But Brittany, you haven't lost me," Amanda whispered. "I've just come to realize that nothing really works out the way we planned." After a pause, she said, "I am jealous of all that wine and cheese, though. Maybe not the film guys. I think I might have written off men for a while."

"I hate when you sound so smart," Brittany told her. "Because you're always so sure of yourself, and I know there's no convincing you otherwise."

As Brittany turned the conversation to other happier things, Grandpa Wes slipped out of his room and stretched his legs toward the window. In the previous week, he'd gotten much stronger, probably as a result of Audrey's "living room walks" with him, which she often said benefited her just as much as him. While Brittany described the "mega insane new Whole Foods" that was now located near her place in Newark, Amanda watched as her grandfather closed his eyes at the splendor of the sun and really took a moment to appreciate the beauty of the morning.

Amanda wanted to always feel this way about the morning.

Just as Amanda got off the phone, Audrey appeared on the bottom step. She beamed at Wes and Amanda and rolled her hands over her enormous belly.

"Another day in the life of my prison-like body," she said with a laugh. "But it's beautiful outside! You can hardly look at the snow. It's too bright. It hurts my eyes."

A cardinal landed on the bird feeder on the other side of the glass from Grandpa Wes. The look on his face was exuberant. He looked like a little kid who'd just discovered candy.

"There he is," Grandpa Wes cooed. "Look at those feathers. My goodness. Can you believe the kind of creatures God cooks up for us?"

Since Grandpa Wes's illness, he had hardly left the house at all. Everyone had been busy; Amanda had been too fearful to go out with him alone. But today felt different. It felt like maybe, he could handle the thick snow, the deep footfalls, and the bright, crisp air.

"Yes. Let's do it," Audrey said boldly after Amanda's suggestion. "I can't spend another day cooped up in this house."

Together, they bundled up. They wore sweaters, thick marshmallow coats, boots, and hats. Amanda watched with cat-like eyes as her grandfather struggled with his right glove, as though he'd lost track of his motions. In a split second, though, he fixed it, lifted his chin, and then winked.

"Let's go see those birds," he announced in a joyful voice.

There was something about the woods right next to the Sheridan house. All of the Sheridan family members knew that this was their little slice of heaven, a space where the snow and the birds and the trees belonged singularly to them. Amanda lifted her eyes to the tree-tops, where the little spindly pieces of wood grew jagged against the bright blue sky. Out there, she felt peace.

"Look!" Grandpa Wes whispered, just loud enough for Audrey and Amanda to hear. He placed his binoculars over his eyes and pointed skyward, where the tiniest yellow-brown bird fluttered. "It's a Ruby-Crowned Kinglet! Look at this little guy. My gosh, he's stunning."

Amanda and Audrey caught one another's eyes as their grandfather continued to gaze at the bird. Their smiles said the same thing: *We would do anything for this man.*

After Grandpa Wes had pointed out a handful of birds and crunched through the snow for a number of minutes, he took a brief pause to lean up against a nearby oak. His smile was tired but serene.

"I can't thank you girls enough for taking me out here," he said.

"We love it just as much as you," Amanda replied.

"I don't know about that," Grandpa Wes said with a soft laugh. "But I really should say, well." He paused, looking reflective. "I should say that I know how much you girls have done for me over the past few weeks. Your mothers are very busy with work and their lives. And I know you two have both come up against quite a difficult season."

His eyes found Audrey, first, as he continued.

"But Audrey. No matter what you're feeling right now about your pregnancy— I should tell you, I don't think I've been this excited about a baby since your own mother was born. I feel included in this, even though I'm the great-grandpa, for goodness sake."

Audrey's eyes grew glossy.

"You two are so much like your mothers, you know? It's uncanny," Grandpa Wes continued. "Amanda and Susan. Audrey and Lola. But you're also your own women. You're building your lives. And it is one of the greater privileges of this old man's life to watch it happen."

He then turned his eyes toward Amanda. Amanda, again on the verge of tears, could hardly breathe.

"I just want to say one thing, Amanda. I don't know what happened in Newark this past week. I just know that one thing about Susan Sheridan is she feels she has to be hard all the time to keep everyone up. I want you to know that we will help you hold yourself up. If you need rest, if you need to grieve, we are here. You don't have to be so strong. Not every day."

* * *

Several hours later, Aunt Kerry came over with sandwiches. Grandpa Wes gave her the dramatic details of every single bird they spotted in the woods until Aunt Kerry looked about as bored as a piece of wood. Amanda and Audrey nestled together on the couch, both quiet. That's when the call from Susan came in.

"What's up, Mom?" Amanda asked.

"Can you get downtown, honey? I have something I want to show you."

Amanda and Audrey borrowed their grandfather's car and eased through the darkening roads to meet Susan downtown. Once there, they found Susan beaming at them from the doorway of the office space they'd just rented. She beckoned them inside, then whipped open the door to reveal an enormous antique desk, built in the mid-1800s, with elaborate carvings on all sides. Amanda placed her hand over her mouth in complete shock.

"What is this, Mom?"

"It's your desk, honey! And look. I had a plaque made up for you," Susan bubbled with happiness as she placed the gold-lined name card on the mahogany desk. "Amanda Harris," she read aloud. "I always thought that sounded like such a strong, beautiful name. And you are the strong, wonderful woman to fill those shoes."

Chapter Twenty-Two

Several days later, Susan rapped her nails across the Sunrise Cove front desk and glared at the door. Natalie had said she would arrive just past eleven so that Susan would be allowed time to eat before putting hours in at the law office. Now, the clock ticked past eleven-thirty, and there hadn't been so much as a text from Natalie.

The door bucked open to reveal Scott. He furrowed his brow and said, "I thought for sure you'd be out of here by now!"

"I know. I was supposed to be." She lifted up on her tiptoes to kiss Scott tenderly and then dropped herself down. "Natalie's late."

Scott nodded. "Which isn't entirely unlike her."

"True. It's just if I'm going to keep up the inn and the law office and everything else, I really need everyone else to pull their weight," Susan said softly. "Otherwise, I might go crazy."

"Said the woman who kept me up all night talking in her sleep," Scott said. He walked around the side of the desk to stand alongside her and throw his arm around her.

158

"I didn't, did I?" Susan breathed. "I'm sorry about that. What did I say?"

"You gave me a recipe for vanilla pudding," Scott said, his smile widening. "And then you asked me to pick up Jake at baseball practice."

"Oops. There's no telling where my psyche was," Susan replied, grinning.

"Just promise me you'll consider fixing your schedule just the slightest bit," Scott suggested as he placed a kiss on her forehead. "I don't want you to overwork yourself, especially so soon after you just got better."

Natalie appeared in the doorway that second and poured out a whole list of excuses, all of which were totally reasonable and easily wiped away. Susan kissed Scott again, grabbed her coat, and hustled out toward downtown. She kept her coat unbuttoned, as somehow, the sun rippled through the bright air to bring forty-degree temperatures, the likes of which they hadn't seen since October.

When Susan appeared in the offices, she found Amanda straight-backed and regal-looking, at the desk she'd purchased for her, with a phone to her ear. She lifted her finger and mouthed, "Just one sec," before she started to scribble something on a pad of paper. Susan jumped through the doorway, overcome with excitement. Already, since Audrey had put up the social media ads, they'd had several calls and pitches for potential clients, including a few off-the-island people up in Falmouth. It was up to Susan and Amanda to decide how much they could take on.

"That sounds great, Sam. Thanks," Amanda said. "I'll call you back with a time shortly."

When Amanda hung up the phone, she grinned up at her mother and did a little dance, still seated. "That was a guy who wants to meet with you about potentially representing his brother," she explained. "DUI."

"Wow. Another one!" Susan said.

"We're reeling them in," Amanda said. "All we can do is try to keep up." After a beat, she continued, "I thought you'd be in before now, actually. Did something happen?"

"No. Natalie got held up," Susan replied. She dropped her things on the desk she'd purchased for herself, which was similarly antique but not as ornate as Amanda's. "I don't know how I can juggle all this. I need to figure something out."

"Maybe I could take on some hours at the Sunrise Cove?" Amanda suggested. "We could juggle both together."

"No. You still have all your classes to take care of," Susan said, tapping a nail to her cheek. "I have to find another option."

* * *

Several hours later, Susan drove over to Edgartown to meet with Sam Fuller, the man who had called the office earlier for a request to meet with Susan about his brother's DUI. She'd left Amanda with a whole stack of paperwork and said, "Make me go to bed early tonight. I swear, I can't see straight anymore."

"Aye, aye, captain," Amanda had said. "Let's keep everyone healthy."

Susan drew the car into the Frosted Delights Bakery parking lot and turned off the engine. Through the glass, she spotted Jennifer Conrad in what looked to be a hilarious conversation with one of her dear friends. Susan was pretty sure she was the nurse, Camilla, but didn't know those girls well enough to confirm. Susan only really knew them as the Sisters of Edgartown.

A handsome, twenty-something guy in what looked to be a second-hand suit appeared at the door of the Frosted Delights. He glanced over the tops of the cars, searching. Susan had a hunch that it was her guy.

"Sam?" she asked as she lifted out of the car and waved a hand.

Sam smiled. It was a deliciously handsome smile, one that assuredly made women his age swoon.

"That's me. You must be Susan Sheridan," he said. He stretched out a hand, and Susan shook it. "Thank you again for meeting me. I really could have met you at the office down-town, but—"

"No worries," Susan said. She hadn't allowed potential clients into the office space yet, as it wasn't fully decorated, and it would build a bad impression. "Besides. There's nothing I like more than a Frosted Delights latte in the middle of the afternoon."

Jennifer and Camilla greeted them warmly and then set to work on their caramel and mint chocolate lattes. Together, Susan and Sam sat near the window while Sam explained the drama of the previous weekend.

"My little brother is a great guy," he explained, with his hands spread out nervously across the table. "But he gets it in his head he's invincible, sometimes."

"Don't we all?" Susan chuckled.

"I guess you have a point," he said. "When he called me from the police station, I wanted to wring his neck, but—"

"But luckily, you held back. Otherwise, we'd have a very different case on our hands," Susan finished for him.

Sam laughed and clicked his nail across the counter. "True. And I don't even really look good in orange."

As their lattes arrived, Sam explained still more of the back-story of Xavier's misstep. "He was out with a few friends, had a few too many drinks, and got pulled over on the way back to Edgartown," he said.

Susan took notes as they went; in her mind, however, this was a pretty simple case. She could have walked through DUI cases in her sleep.

"Okay. Well. In these kinds of cases, there's no way not to prove that he didn't do it, obviously," Susan told him.

"Obviously."

"But we can walk back the charges a bit, reduce the fine he has to pay, that kind of thing."

"Great. Yes. That's exactly what I need," Sam said. "We just came out here a little over a month ago, and I haven't been able to nail down a job yet."

"Oh? So you aren't an islander, then?"

"No. We're from Oklahoma, actually," Sam replied. "Far, far from home."

"What brings you all the way out here? It's pretty strange that you're here in the winter and not an islander. Vineyard winters can be brutal."

Sam gestured out toward the melting snow and said, "Today is a beautiful winter's day, actually. It'll be spring soon."

"Yes. Yes, you're right. It is," Susan agreed. "But really. Oklahoma? I'm curious." She flipped the folder closed and crossed her fingers beneath her chin. It was a rare thing that she allowed herself even a few moments of interesting conversation. Normally, she had to rush off.

"Well, tell you the truth, Xavier and I's parents died a few years back," Sam said.

Susan's heart dropped. "Oh. I'm so sorry to hear that."

"Yeah. Well. It wasn't a fun ride for either of us. They died in a car accident, which only exacerbated my anger toward my brother's drunk driving, but that is another story. Anyway, I had a full ride for a master's in tourism management and hospitality out east, and I dragged Xavier out here with me. My program ended at the end of last year, and we were both wicked sick of Boston."

"Ha. Wicked," Susan said, mocking the fake accent.

"Exactly," Sam said. "We're from a small town, and we wanted to find a place that we could call home and lay some

162

roots down. We heard of Martha's Vineyard, and we popped over one day, found a little rental house, and never left. That said, the hospitality doesn't pick up till May or June, I guess, and we're running low on funds. Now, Xavier got arrested, and I'm starting to second-guess the whole plan."

Susan's heart swelled with pity for this man, who had only just grown out of his own boyhood. "That's awful," she said. "Really. It's too many things for a guy like yourself to take on at once. And this is coming from someone with her own share of heartaches. I hope you won't blame your brother too much for what happened."

Susan thought of Christine and Lola and the way they'd interacted together earlier the previous summer. It had been difficult initially for them all to forgive one another for the stress and hardships and sadness they'd put on one another. Now, in the wake of forgiveness, it all felt so simple.

"I know. I don't want to," Sam said. "I just can't get it out of my head. I'm killing myself, trying to get a job, and well..." He blinked several times, then added, "I don't mean to bore you. This is completely outside of your job description. You've done enough. Thank you."

The words flew out of Susan's lips swiftly.

"I actually operate an inn in Oak Bluffs," she announced.

"Oh?" Sam's eyes glittered strangely, as though he didn't dare to hope for whatever it was she suggested.

"Yes. Now that I've opened this law office, I'm in desperate need of a helping hand around the inn. Someone with your background would be very beneficial to our family business. I wonder if you would like to stop by tomorrow afternoon for an interview?"

Sam looked shocked at her sudden offer, but then excitement filled his face. He stuttered for a second and then said, "Are you sure?"

"Of course," Susan replied. She stood and stretched her

hand out between them for him to shake. "You sound uniquely qualified and besides, I like the idea that you came to Martha's Vineyard on a whim, without ever having been here before. Maybe the island called to you like a siren. Who knows?"

Chapter Twenty-Three

Amanda hustled out of her bedroom to find Grandpa Wes and Audrey seated at the kitchen table. Grandpa Wes had his large hands wrapped around a coffee mug while Audrey read from her phone.

"When did the Civil War start?"

"April 1861," Grandpa Wes returned.

"And when did the Berlin Wall fall?"

"November 9, 1989. I remember that like it was yesterday," Grandpa Wes stated, lifting his mug to take a sip.

"Who was the thirteenth president of the United States?" Audrey asked as though he hadn't added his own anecdote.

Grandpa Wes furrowed his brow for a long time. Amanda stepped delicately around the table to gather her things. After a long pause, she said, "I don't think anyone knows who the thirteenth president was, Aud—"

"Millard Fillmore," Grandpa Wes blurted out just then. "It has to be him."

Audrey snapped her fingers gleefully, then turned and then smiled at Amanda. "He's still got it! Sharp as a whip!"

Amanda rolled her eyes playfully. "Whatever. What's this all about?"

"Grandpa told me he could remember basically everything except five minutes ago, so I wanted to test him," Audrey explained. "You should have seen him sweat over a question about Japan, but he got it! Grandpa, I really didn't know you were such a scholar."

Grandpa Wes grinned inwardly, clearly pleased with himself. Obviously, the dementia hadn't run its course through him. Not the full course, anyway.

"Where you off to?"

"I'm headed to the law office," Amanda answered. "I pre-made your lunches for the day; they're in the fridge. Audrey, you just have to stick them in the oven at 400 degrees for about fifteen minutes. And Audrey, you're still meeting Aunt Lola, Aunt Christine, my mom, and I, right?"

"At six-thirty. Yep," Audrey said. "If I can waddle my way over there."

"Don't worry about it if you can't make it," Amanda told her. "We'd just love your company, obviously."

"And I'd love to see a sight outside of this room," Audrey retorted sarcastically.

"Are you suggesting the company leaves something to be desired?" Grandpa Wes asked.

Audrey arched her brow, placed her phone on the table between them, and said, "Come on, Grandpa. Quiz me next."

"With this thing?" Grandpa Wes asked as he lifted the phone. "You know I don't know my way around this new technology."

Amanda headed out the door and made her way toward downtown Oak Bluffs. As she marched, her boots sloshed through the melted snow and dabbed at the mud beneath. How was it possible that it was already February 22? How was it possible that an entire month had passed since she had been stood up at the altar? Time had always passed by quickly, but this was ridiculous.

Just last night, Brittany had texted Amanda with a screenshot of Chris's Instagram photo.

BRITTANY: Um, can you tell me why Chris is in Spain right now?

Amanda hadn't known what to answer. She hadn't expected the photo. Chris was on a beach with a drink in hand and a larger-than-life smile plastered between his cheeks. He didn't look like the Chris she had once known, but he did look happier.

At the law office, Amanda found her mother wrestling a newly purchased potted plant into the foyer. Amanda hurriedly jumped toward her to help her place it directly to the side of a gorgeous painting they'd also recently chosen from a local artist. Susan snapped her hands together and analyzed the sight— the beginnings of their "artistic" foyer.

"I think it looks pretty good. Almost good enough for clients," Susan stated.

"Almost," Amanda replied.

For the rest of the morning and afternoon, Amanda busied herself with schoolwork and paperwork for the law office. Her mother popped in and out, meeting clients and helping out at the Sunrise Cove. She had mentioned that she'd hired someone to operate the front desk to allow her more time at the law offices, which Amanda was grateful for. Still, it was every bit like her mother to burn the candle at both ends.

The day flew by. Audrey texted a few times with questions about the lunch she had prepared them (how long to bake it in the oven again?) and whether or not she knew where the chessboard was (as it was apparently beneficial for dementia patients to play chess). Around three, Audrey announced that Aunt Kerry had arrived with chocolate chip cookies and that she planned to eat all of them herself. "I only have a few weeks left of this pregnancy, and I have to milk it for all it's worth, right?"

Amanda's mind couldn't have been further from the idea of babies and marriage. It surprised her, sometimes, when she awoke in the middle of the night and felt horrible and frightened and alone. Her eyes scanned the bed beside her for some sign of Chris, even as her mind came back to the realization that she was no longer engaged; she no longer lived in Newark, and that she was someone else, now.

Susan and Amanda bundled up and headed back to the Sunrise Cove to meet Aunt Lola, Aunt Christine, and Audrey for dinner at the bistro. As they walked, they nearly stumbled headlong into Everett, Charlotte, and her daughter, Rachel, who laughed as they traipsed through the center of town.

"Hey, you three!" Susan called.

Charlotte beamed and waved. "Where are you girls headed to?"

"Sunrise Cove," Susan and Amanda said in unison.

"I should have known," Charlotte said. Her eyes turned toward Amanda. Within them, Amanda hated to see that Charlotte did, in some ways, pity Amanda and all she'd been through on that horrible, fateful day. "Amanda, I'm so glad you're still on the island."

Everett leaned in and said, "She says that to me every day. But it's not like I'd ever go back to LA."

Amanda laughed gratefully for a moment, then allowed the silence to fill the air between them. After a moment, Susan said, "Well, we have to meet the girls," and then turned back.

Just before Charlotte left Amanda's sight, however, Amanda rushed back and tapped her on the shoulder. Charlotte turned. Her eyes looked heavy, as though she wanted to apologize for what she'd said. But before she could say a single word, Amanda said, "I really loved the wedding you put together, Charlotte. It was so beautiful."

Charlotte dropped her chin to her chest. She looked on the verge of tears.

"Really. I just wanted to thank you for all your hard work. And also say that, well." Amanda laughed lightly. "As stupid as this sounds, I really do think I'll get married someday. To someone. Who knows who? But when that day comes, I would really like you to be the one who plans it again."

"You know I'll be there for you, no matter what," Charlotte said.

* * *

Amanda and Susan met Lola, Christine, and Audrey at the bistro just past six-thirty. Already, Christine and Lola had a bottle of merlot popped, and Audrey had waded her way through half of the basket of garlic bread. Lola and Christine hopped up for big, boisterous hugs, while Audrey just waved a tired hand and said, "I barely made it here in one piece. This baby just kicks and kicks and kicks."

"I told her she did the same," Lola said. "I knew she was going to be a spitfire. And now, look at her! All grown up and complaining non-stop."

They ordered salads from Ronnie, along with another basket of garlic bread. Amanda turned to wave at Zach as he walked out of the kitchen. He winked just before he bent to speak with a table of customers. Amanda's heart swelled. Soon, she would be able to watch Zach and Christine and Audrey wade through the waters of "parenthood." It was difficult to know what that would look like.

When Ronnie placed the basket of garlic bread at the table, Audrey reached for her pocket and discovered that she'd forgotten her phone in the coat room.

"Don't get up. I'll grab it for you!" Amanda offered.

"No, no. I need to stretch my legs," Audrey said. "I feel

uncomfortable in one place for too long." Slowly, she moved up from the table and walked toward the hallway, which led out toward the foyer and the coatroom.

After Audrey disappeared, Lola's eyes bore into Amanda. "Is she really doing okay?" she demanded. "She's stopped telling me stuff. She seems...distant."

Amanda shrugged. "I think she's just focused on the next few weeks. Probably she's freaking out and just needs space. I think Grandpa Wes is helping."

Lola and Christine exchanged glances. Susan sipped her wine. Amanda felt bad about having this discussion without Audrey at the table. Her allegiance was to Audrey above all other people, it felt like.

"I just hope she knows we're here for her if she needs help," Lola said. "She's my daughter, and I know she's going through a lot, but—"

Suddenly, from the depths of the coatroom came a blood-curdling scream.

Amanda leaped from her chair. Later, when she thought about it, she thought maybe she blacked out as she raced toward the coatroom. She was faster than the others, by fifteen feet, maybe more, and found herself at Audrey's feet, alongside a tall man who looked to be in his twenties. Amanda had never seen him before. Immediately, the man dropped down beside Audrey and said, "Ma'am? Ma'am, my name is Sam Fuller. Ma'am, are you going into labor?"

Audrey's eyes were watery, and she looked terrified. She stretched her hands over her stomach and peered up at Amanda while the handsome man remained on his knees beside her.

"Audrey?" Amanda murmured. She curled up beside her, across from Sam Fuller, and clasped Audrey's hand. "What happened?"

Audrey shook her head back and forth. "I don't know. It felt like a contraction. It was a sharp, tightening pain that shot across my stomach and then traveled to my lower back. It took my breath away."

Susan, Lola, and Christine appeared in the coatroom seconds later, all gasping for breath. They analyzed the scene as Lola dropped down to sit at Audrey's feet. She reached up to grip Audrey's other hand and said, "Do you think you're going into labor, baby?"

It was much, much too soon for anything like that, and they all knew it.

Of course, crazier things had happened.

"I don't know," Audrey admitted. She sounded like she wanted to be sarcastic but didn't have the strength left. "I've never gone into labor before, Mom."

"More than likely, it's Braxton Hicks contractions. They're false labor pains. It's completely normal, honey," Lola explained, giving her daughter a reassuring smile.

Minutes passed. Sam Fuller stood up to allow Lola a place next to Audrey, who still refused to get up from the ground. Amanda watched Sam trace a path out toward the foyer again; he looked anxious, wide-eyed, and eager to help out if Audrey let out another screech of alarm.

On instinct, Amanda followed him out into the foyer. Christine crept into position next to Audrey as she left and whispered, "Do you want to get up? I can drive you back home. You can even stay with me tonight if you want to."

Amanda didn't wait to hear Audrey's response. She knew that Audrey was under too much pressure as it was.

Back out in the foyer, Amanda watched as Sam returned back to the Sunrise Cove front desk and began to jot notes in the booklet her mother ordinarily used. As Amanda walked past, Sam lifted his head and said, "I'm glad you came to my rescue. I can't imagine helping someone give birth during my first week at the new job."

Amanda laughed, surprising herself. Something in her belly fluttered strangely.

"That's actually the first test we give out here at the Sunrise Cove to new employees," she replied. "If you can deliver the baby, you can stay on staff."

"Wow. That's tough," Sam said. "I guess I should have paid more attention in biology class."

Amanda's smile widened. *Am I flirting with this guy? Probably not, right? I don't remember how to flirt anymore.*

"How do you like working here so far?"

Sam tilted his head. "You know, I met Susan Sheridan just a few days ago, and I had this weird feeling about her. She just seemed so warm and welcoming. And when she told me about this potential job, I thought maybe, just maybe, she was my guardian angel. Although hey. It's still my first week. I have plenty of time to mess up."

"Plenty," Amanda agreed. "We have our eyes on you at all times."

"We?" Sam asked. His smile was dangerously attractive now.

"I'm Susan Sheridan's daughter. And intern," Amanda introduced herself.

"Ah. So you're second-in-command of all things," he stated, giving her a lop-sided grin.

"You could say that."

"Interesting and good to know. I'll make sure to stay on your good side from here on out," Sam said.

At that moment, Audrey, Lola, Christine, and Susan reappeared in the foyer. Audrey brushed a strand of hair from her sweaty forehead and said, "Sorry about the chaos. You know I like to create whatever drama I can."

"So no baby?" Amanda asked.

Audrey shook her head. "Nope. She's staying in there till I tell her to. Or else."

Chapter Twenty-Four

When the Sheridan sisters, Amanda, and Audrey, arrived back at the Sheridan house that evening, it was decided that Audrey take Amanda's bedroom downstairs.

"I don't want you to push yourself too hard these next few weeks," Lola said, using that extra firm tone that meant, *I am your mother, and you will listen to me.*

But they didn't have to work too hard to convince Audrey that she needed rest. After she'd settled into the bed that had been Amanda's, Amanda perched at the edge of her bed and squeezed her hand while Audrey's eyes closed.

"I can't get over how painful that felt and how much it scared me," Audrey whispered to Amanda.

"I bet that's just what it feels like to have a contraction," Amanda said. "There's no way to know until it happens to you."

"Yeah. I guess I just thought since I'm so young and, you know, in the prime of health and all that, that maybe it wouldn't hurt so much?"

Amanda laughed lightly. "I don't think that's how it works."

"Figures," Audrey said.

"I'll bring you breakfast in bed tomorrow, before I head off to the office," Amanda told her. "Christine already said she'd come by at lunch to make sure you and Grandpa are taken care of."

Audrey buzzed her lips and shifted slightly beneath the sheets. Obviously, she didn't adore all the attention. Not like this.

"Thanks, Mandy. Sorry, I was so dramatic and ruined dinner," she said. "I promise, by this time next year, I'll be out of your hair and back doing keg stands at Penn State."

"That's the spirit," Amanda said. "Make your baby proud."

At this, they both burst into raucous laughter, so loud that Susan rushed in to say, "Grandpa Wes only just fell asleep, girls. Can you please keep it down?"

Back in the living room, Amanda stepped into a quiet but intense conversation about Audrey's health.

"I did struggle with those last few weeks," Lola admitted.

"Mom always said she struggled with you, too," Susan said to Lola. "Maybe it's just something in the genes?"

"I don't want her to worry," Christine murmured. "I think that stress would only exacerbate things."

"You're right," Susan said. "Let's just keep it light and simple. I think it's smart she's downstairs now. Charlotte has also agreed to stop by tomorrow morning since Amanda and I have clients to take care of. Thank goodness I hired that young man at the Sunrise Cove. He has already changed a few of the systems to reflect what he learned in school, and I couldn't be more pleased."

"He's certainly handsome," Christine said with a funny smile.

Susan laughed. "I didn't hire him because of his looks, believe it or not."

"I would have," Lola grinned. "Although you know I'm the vain one of the group."

That night, Susan headed off to Scott's. Before she left, she explained tomorrow's schedule to Amanda. "I'll be in the office around one, I guess. I have to train Sam on a few more things before he takes over completely."

"Sounds good," Amanda said. "I'll see you there. And I'll bring you a salad!"

"You're a dream, honey," Susan replied. "See you there, future partner."

The following morning, Amanda delivered breakfast to both Audrey and her grandfather, just as Charlotte and Everett arrived. Everett, apparently, had to head off to New York that evening for a photography gig, so he had agreed to help out at the Sheridan house before his departure. Charlotte hugged Amanda close and said, "Thanks for asking me to help. I've been so bogged down with wedding planning for the upcoming season. It'll be good to do something that doesn't involve lace and candles and flowers and evil bridezillas."

"We appreciate it," Amanda said in a low voice. "Audrey has had some false labor, and we just don't fully expect her to watch over Grandpa when she's dealing with so much."

"I totally get it," Charlotte said.

As Amanda donned her spring jacket (again, another forty-something degree day!), she noticed that her mother had left her notebook on the counter. Something in the back of her mind told her that maybe Susan just didn't need it that day. But another part of the back of her mind saw it as an opportunity.

Amanda walked to the Sunrise Cove Inn in a kind of hazy zone of optimism. She wasn't totally sure where the feeling came from or even how she'd built it up in the midst of so much pain and heartache. Before she knew what she'd done, she found herself at the front desk of the Sunrise Cove Inn, right directly in front of that handsome and hilarious young man, Sam Fuller.

"Hey there!" he greeted her. "Your mom just went over to the Bistro to talk to Zach."

Amanda hated to sense a blush creeping up over her neck and through her cheeks. She swallowed as she placed the notebook on the counter. "Mom left this at our place," she informed him. "I just wanted to make sure she had it for the day."

Does that sound like the most made-up excuse to come down here, or what?

"Cool!" Sam said. "I'll make sure it finds its way to her. Apparently, Zach had some kind of problem with an order, and she has to ease out a few wrinkles. On her way there, she said, 'Congratulations, Sam. This is the kind of job you'll have to do next week, but I'll take care of it for now.' Sounds like lots of fun!"

Amanda laughed outright. "I don't envy you."

"Well, I don't envy all the law you have in that head of yours," Sam replied. "I guess you stick to the law, and I'll stick to the hospitality."

Christine appeared in the little hallway between the bistro and the Sunrise Cove. In her hands, she carried a large tray of what looked like four different kinds of pastries.

"Amanda!" she greeted. "I didn't know you were coming in today."

"Mom left something at the house," Amanda said— again, this lie that wasn't quite a lie. "I had to bring it in."

"Perfect. Then you have time to try one of the new pastries I've been working on," Christine said. "I was inspired a bit by what they have going on at the Frosted Delights Bakery in Edgartown."

"I'm glad you're here," Sam said to Amanda. "Christine has been forcing me to try all her new creations alone, and I swear I've already gained a few pounds since my first day."

Christine laughed. "Better you than me, kiddo. Your metabolism can handle it. Mine can't!"

Sam lifted the knife Christine had brought and tenderly sliced through the pastries. With each movement of his knife, creamy lemon or raspberry or blackberry goop came out of the crispy dough.

"Christine, you've outdone yourself," Sam said as he closed his eyes on the first bite. "Man. It's fantastic. Amanda, you have to try this one."

Amanda lifted a square of the lemon flavor and chewed slowly. Crispy, lemony, and sweet with the slightest hint of sour — it was complex and not too overwhelming, the kind of thing you could get addicted to.

"Aunt Christine, what the heck!" Amanda said, her mouth full.

Sam's eyes found hers as he nodded. Amanda wasn't fully sure if her excitement for the pastry was tied up in the pastry itself or in Sam's eyes. He was sure easy to look at.

"Well, anyway. I have to run." Amanda finally mustered the strength to say it a few minutes later. "Make sure Mom gets this notebook, okay?"

"Take a pastry with you!" Christine wrapped the caramel-flavored one up and chased Amanda to the door. When she reached it, she winked as she slipped the package into Amanda's hands. "I hope you stop by soon. I have plenty more pastries to make you taste-test."

Christine's tone was very much like: *I know exactly what you're up to, Miss Amanda Harris.* But she didn't call her out on it.

* * *

Amanda found herself drawn to the Sunrise Cove several times over the next week. She dropped off lunch for her mother and

Scott; she stopped by for a drink with Aunt Christine after a long day of school and work; and she found herself committed to trying all of Christine's newest pastry flavors, usually alongside Sam. In fact, she and Sam had drawn up a little chart for their favorite flavors, which they kept hanging in the office.

"You know, my grandfather and grandmother used to share this office when they handled the Sunrise Cove together," Amanda told him as he placed "Lime Pastry" in last place on the chart.

"Your mom told me," he said with a funny smile. "I can't believe I'm involved in such a big part of the Sheridan family history."

"To be honest, it almost ran itself into the ground last year," Amanda said.

"Well, it'll run itself into the ground again if Christine gets any more ideas about lime pastries," Sam replied, just loud enough for Christine to hear as she passed by the office.

"Hey! I don't like that tone of voice," Christine called out. After a pause, she added, "But you're right. That one was a total disaster. Total misfire. My apologies."

Sam drew his watch up toward his face and said, "Ah! Six o'clock."

Amanda's heart did a somersault. She knew that usually, Sam got off work at six. From various things he had said, she had picked up that he normally spent his evenings with his brother, who was still pretty down after the DUI situation.

But tonight, he lifted his eyes toward Amanda's and said, "I don't feel like going home yet. Do you want to go to that saloon on Main Street? I've been meaning to grab a drink there since we got to the island."

What. The. Heck.

Is this a date?

Amanda's lips parted. For a moment, she forgot how to speak.

"I mean, only if you don't have plans. I know you have a zillion things to take care of," Sam said quickly. "With Audrey and your grandfather and everything. I—"

"Oh, no. Everything's taken care of today," Amanda replied, waving her hand. "I'd love to have a drink. Sounds nice."

Amanda hadn't been out on a first date since the age of eighteen— not that this was a date, exactly. She had to remind herself that over and over again. Still, as she donned her coat, another thought struck her: *Chris never made me laugh the way Sam makes me laugh.* No. She had to shove these thoughts away.

She'd only just gotten left at the altar, for goodness sake.

Amanda and Sam walked over to the saloon side-by-side. It seemed like Amanda always had something to say to him; sometimes, she felt she would never run out of things to say. By the time they'd reached the saloon, they'd already erupted into three bouts of gut-busting laughter. And by the time they had ordered their first round of drinks, Amanda had thought, at least once, *Wow. He would make the best boyfriend ever.*

"How do you like Martha's Vineyard so far?" Amanda asked him while taking the first sip of her wine. She tried not to focus on how beautiful his eyes were.

"I love it!" Sam said. "Actually, it was always kind of a pipe dream to live on an island. It's been a really weird few years, and I guess I never thought that Xavier and I would figure anything out. You know, I imagined us always living in that crummy apartment in Boston and barely making rent. Now, well—" He gestured out toward the boisterous bar, the beautiful exterior of Main Street, and then toward Amanda. "My life has totally flipped around. I sometimes have to pinch myself."

Amanda pressed her lips together. There was so much of her own feelings tied up in what he'd just said. It didn't feel time to tell him all that, though. It was better to linger on happier things.

Their conversation bubbled and popped for the next few hours. Amanda's heart floated into her throat as he ordered them a second and then the third round of drinks. "Don't worry. These are on me," he told her. "I haven't been out in a while."

On instinct, Amanda checked her phone and immediately said aloud, "Oh my gosh! Did you know it's ten at night?" Apparently, they'd managed to talk to one another for the previous four hours. She had hardly noticed the time passing.

Sam chuckled and dropped his face into his hands. "That's crazy. I guess time flies when you're having fun."

"I guess so."

They locked eyes for a long time. Finally, Amanda said, "Well, I guess I'd better get back."

Sam nodded. "Me too. I have an early morning, and you have all those people to take care of back home."

"Right."

Amanda watched as Sam paid. He tipped the bartender forty percent and then winked as he got up. Together, they entered the chill of the late February night. Amanda prayed for him to wrap his arm around her, but she also hoped that he wouldn't. Her feelings were so complex; her heart remained so bruised.

As they walked toward the edge of Main Street, silence fell around them. Sam placed his hands in his pockets and said, "You know, I haven't met anyone like you before."

Amanda felt the words like a punch in the stomach. "I haven't met anyone like you, either."

Silence fell again. Amanda marveled that pain and happiness were like cousins, so closely linked.

"Maybe your mom told you, but I lost my parents a few

years ago," Sam finally admitted. "And it's been a really hard road since then."

Of course, Susan had explained his backstory, but hearing it from Sam's lips instead felt unique and difficult and also necessary.

"That sounds so awful, Sam," Amanda whispered. "I am so sorry."

Sam shrugged. "It still feels raw, especially now taking care of my little brother. But I'm trying all the time to get better."

Amanda sniffed. After a long moment, she said, "It doesn't compare, not at all, but I was just um...left at the altar about a month ago. A month ago, I thought I was going to spend the rest of my life with my fiancé. And now? Now, I don't know what's next for me."

Sam's eyes were wide like saucers. "Wow. That guy doesn't know what he lost. And it's not so, so different. You lost someone you loved."

She blushed a little before saying, "I really did."

"And it's hell, isn't it?"

"Yes," Amanda whispered. "It's hell."

Sam gestured out again toward Main Street. "But look at us, huh? There's still so much to live for. And I think, well, that you have to be brave enough to just live life to the fullest. It's the only thing to do."

Amanda nodded. Again, they held one another's gaze. Finally, she said, "One thing I've really thought about since Chris left me is how long life is, actually. It's such a blessing. You can make decisions and change your mind. You can build new eras for yourself. You can become someone totally different."

And maybe, just maybe, you can find new love.

"Life is long," Sam whispered. "Well said."

Then, beautifully, without letting another moment pass, Sam pressed his lips against Amanda's cheek. The motion was so tender, so polite, so kind, and so loving that it nearly broke Amanda's heart all over again. When it ended, he leaned back and said, "I am so glad to have met you, Amanda. And I hope we might be able to do this again, sooner than later."

Amanda and Sam parted ways that night. Amanda walked through the chill and the dark with her head in the clouds. With every step she took, she dared herself to believe in something more than heartache. She dared herself to have hope again. She dared herself to feel as hard as she could, for as long as she was alive.

It was the only thing she could do.

Chapter Twenty-Five

Susan awoke on the final Saturday of February. She rolled over beneath the rough sheets and placed her chin on Scott's broad chest. He groaned quietly beneath her as she eased against him. She could still feel whatever dreamland he existed in; his eyes slipped back and forth beneath his eyelids as he engaged with other sights, other colors.

Goodness, how she loved him.

She slipped out from the sheets a few minutes later. She donned her slippers and her robe and headed to the little kitchen, where she brewed coffee and watched as the sunlight played out across the Vineyard Sound. Due to Sam and Natalie's schedules, she didn't have to go into the Sunrise Cove that morning, that afternoon, or even that evening. She had no meetings scheduled as a criminal lawyer. All she had was this peace. How grateful she was for it.

When Scott awoke, he walked in a slumber toward her and placed a kiss on her lips. "I'm going to make bacon and eggs and biscuits," she told him, and he groaned with pleasure. "Just sit down. I'll have it all ready for you in no time."

"Susan Sheridan, if I hadn't already asked you to marry me, maybe I'd do it again right now," Scott said as he rubbed his eyes.

With two massive platters of food spread out before them, Susan and Scott dug in. Through bites and laughter, Susan acknowledged that they'd both worked too hard the previous months.

"I'm sorry about that," she said. "And actually, I thought that maybe, we could hire someone else to work with you at the inn on all the handyman stuff. I know you want more time to go see your son. And besides that, we really need to start planning."

Scott arched his brow. "Planning what?"

Susan shrugged and playfully nudged him. "You know... our wedding."

Scott's face brightened. He placed another kiss on her cheek and said, "Let's set a date. Right now."

"Come on. You know I already have one in mind," Susan said.

"I should have known."

"What about June 19?"

"It sounds perfect," Scott beamed. "And just about a year after your big arrival back to the Vineyard."

"Exactly," Susan winked. "And what a year it's been."

Susan spent a blissful morning and afternoon with Scott: eating, kissing, cuddling, and watching the waves. Mid-way through the afternoon, the Sheridan sisters, Amanda, and Audrey, agreed via text message to meet at the Sheridan house for "sister time." Overwhelmed with all the love she had in her life, Susan showered and dressed and kissed Scott goodbye.

"My girls need me," she told him, smiling from ear to ear. She couldn't remember the last time she had been this happy.

* * *

When Susan arrived back at the Sheridan house, Audrey, Amanda, and Wes marched out of the damp yet bright woods, all with enormous smiles. Her father flung an arm around Susan's shoulder and said, "You should have seen this heron. Audrey spotted him first, and we all got a great look at him through the binoculars."

"My three bird watchers," Susan said.

Christine appeared in the back doorway and waved. "We just popped a bottle of wine, Susan! You're just in time."

They piled inside to find Lola and Christine sitting with a huge platter of newly-baked pastries. The light hit the front porch beautifully, and Susan suggested they bundle up and sit outside to watch the water and feel the last of the late-winter sun rays. Before they managed to get everyone outside, however, Grandpa Wes sat in an armchair and was completely passed out.

"I guess we wore him out," Amanda said.

"That's a good thing. He's probably having dreams about the woods and his birds," Susan suggested.

Outside, the three Sheridan sisters, Amanda, and Audrey, sat, wrapped up in thick blankets. The wine was poured for Susan and Amanda while Audrey sipped on a hot chocolate. For a long time, a comfortable silence stretched between them. In the distance, a large boat hovered across the frigid Vineyard Sound. Someday very soon, the waters would be warm once again, and the island would come alive as the population grew with tourists.

"We set a date for the wedding," Susan heard herself say.

"Oh my gosh! I thought you would never get around to setting a date," Lola said.

"June 19," Susan announced, beaming ear to ear. "I'll have

to talk to Charlotte. I want the whole thing to be small, you know. Nothing too big."

"Phew. We'll have to get something really cute for the baby to wear," Christine said, mostly to Audrey.

"Something very frilly and girly. Maybe pink," Audrey added.

"You're still so sure it's a girl," Christine said. They hadn't opted to find out the gender.

"Aunt Christine, I've told you and Zach again and again. This baby is a girl. I refuse to give birth to a boy," Audrey said, chuckling lightly.

Over the next minutes, they chatted excitedly about the baby, about Audrey's health, and about what the baby might look like, based on their brief Facebook stalking of the baby-daddy. Audrey laughed again and said, "He just looks like some random guy now. I have zero emotional attachment to even the concept of him."

"It's funny how that happens, isn't it?" Lola said. "I can remember tons of guys that I was obsessed with, who I now don't remember the last names of. Time is funny like that."

Amanda hadn't spoken in several minutes. There seemed to be a dark cloud over her. Susan opened her lips to ask her a question— anything to bring her back to the world, but Christine beat her to it.

"You've been spending an awful lot of time at the Sunrise Cove, Miss Amanda," Christine said.

Amanda's cheeks burned tomato-red. "I mean, it's our family's inn. That's not so crazy, is it?"

Christine gave a light shrug. "No. I guess not." She sipped her wine, her eyes sparkling, as she said, "It's just that, you know. You and Sam have struck up quite a friendship."

Susan's jaw dropped. How had she missed this?!

Amanda's cheeks turned a deep crimson. "It's nice to have a new friend on the island. It's just been you guys and Audrey since I moved here. No offense, but I needed something a little different."

Her smile stretched wider, proof that she teased them.

Still, there was something in Amanda's eyes. Something that told Susan: Amanda would be all right.

Even if this crush meant nothing to her in the end— having a crush on a boy meant something. It meant she hadn't given up quite yet. It meant that maybe she was getting over Chris.

"That sun," Lola finally said, seeming to sense that Amanda wanted a change of conversation. "It reminds me so much of spring."

"Me too," Susan said. "I can feel it... all this excitement for the year ahead."

"It's crazy how much has changed," Christine said. "I can't believe I haven't been back to New York since the summer."

"Do you miss it?" Lola asked.

Christine shook her head. "Not at all. Do you miss Boston?"

"No." Lola laughed outright. "You couldn't pay me to move back to Boston."

Amanda and Susan caught one another's eye. Again, Amanda blushed.

"I don't think you could pay me to be married to Chris, either," Amanda said suddenly. "It now feels like the worst idea in the history of ideas. Like maybe I never knew him at all."

They huddled closer together. Susan wrapped her arm around her daughter and dropped her head across her shoulder.

After a long moment of silence, Amanda spoke.

"During that week before my wedding, I worked really hard at writing my vows. Maybe for reasons that are obvious now, I struggled to know what to say to this man I was supposed to love and cherish for the rest of my life. I wrote draft after draft, even in the hours leading up to the ceremony that never happened. They didn't sound like anything. They sounded boring and flat and stupid."

"Amanda, nothing you've ever done is stupid," Lola said.

Amanda chuckled. "Maybe, maybe not. But in any case, I never got to read those vows. And I'm glad about that because they were kind of a lie. They're such a weird contrast to everything I've done since then. And being here with all of you and starting this business with Mom. Cooking and cleaning and loving as hard as I can. I realized it wasn't just going through the motions. It was real. It was more real than anything I've done in years."

Amanda's eyes brimmed with tears. "Anyway, maybe that all sounds silly to you, but I just wanted to say that I've never felt this way before. I'm hopeful for my future. Whatever happens next, I know it will be better than anything I could have planned for myself— no matter how many lists I might have written. I guess, in a way, these are my vows. These words right here. To you four— the Sheridan girls. I love you forever."

Susan's heart swelled as the sun dipped toward the glowing line of the Vineyard Sound's horizon. Soon, their lives would shift toward another future of what-ifs and fears and doubts and endless buckets of love. But in these moments, as they held one another close, she knew they could handle anything that came their way. Nothing would ever be the way it had been; nothing ever turned out the way they had planned. And truly, it was better this way. Their lives overflowed with love. They were overjoyed with it. And soon, it would be spring.

Coming Next

Next in the series

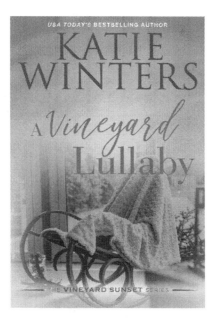

Other Books by Katie

The Vineyard Sunset Series

Secrets of Mackinac Island Series

Sisters of Edgartown Series

A Katama Bay Series

A Mount Desert Island Series

A Nantucket Sunset Series

Connect with Katie Winters

BookBub
Facebook
Newsletter

To receive exclusive updates from Katie Winters please sign up
to be on her Newsletter!
CLICK HERE TO SUBSCRIBE

Made in United States
Orlando, FL
07 March 2023